KU-072-814

BOLTON LIBRARIES

BT21510040

Law Killers

John Carter is on top of the world as the sheriff in Destiny, one of the most law-abiding towns in the south-western states. But almost from the moment that Rebecca Seymour, the attractive, temperamental Pinkerton agent, arrives in town, he is in trouble.

Now he's a target for unknown assailants who want him injured – or dead – and they're not too fussy about their methods. Fleeing for his life, Carter goes from the jaws of danger into even more peril when he ends up in the clutches of the Sullivan clan who have many reasons to hate him.

Reunited with Rebecca, and with the support of a rookie deputy, Carter is finally cornered and knows that he has to come out fighting, or everything he has fought for will be lost in a welter of corruption, destruction and murder.

Law Killers

Alex Frew

A Black Horse Western

ROBERT HALE

© Alex Frew 2019
First published in Great Britain 2019

ISBN 978-0-7198-2971-0

The Crowood Press
The Stable Block
Crowood Lane
Ramsbury
Marlborough
Wiltshire SN8 2HR

www.bhwesterns.com

Robert Hale is an imprint
of The Crowood Press

The right of Alex Frew to be identified as
author of this work has been asserted by him
in accordance with the Copyright, Designs and
Patents Act 1988

All rights reserved. No part of this publication may be
reproduced or transmitted in any form or by any means,
electronic or mechanical, including photocopying, recording,
or any information storage and retrieval system, without
permission in writing from the publishers.

Typeset by
Derek Doyle & Associates, Shaw Heath
Printed and bound in Great Britain by
4Bind Ltd, Stevenage, SG1 2XT

CHAPTER ONE

Sheriff John Carter came into his office. It was not the biggest workplace to be found in the state of Kansas, yet Destiny, on the south west of the state, was the biggest town in the district. He ignored the two sullen men who occupied two of the cells attached to his office. These were Jonas Burrows and Dick Lambert, both of whom, if only he knew it, were to feature prominently later on in his life. Nor was he to know that life as he had known it was about to turn upside down and inside out, too.

Not that Carter was too bothered about life at that moment. He had a roomy office, and not one, but two desks. One was just a normal desk with a drawer, behind which he would sit on a bentwood chair, and this was placed in front of the main office window.

The other desk, on the far side of the office, presented a different picture altogether. It was made of teak and was a dark red with golden overtones that gave it an inner glow in the light from the main window to which it sat sideways, facing the faded yellow paint of the plain wall. This desk had been tailor-made by a master craftsman called Jeb Whithorn, and it had been a present to Carter from the grateful businessmen of the town. Neither was the surface just flat, because on each side of the desk was a stack of pigeon holes into which could be placed bills, depositions and correspondence. At the back was another built-in wooden tidy in which could be placed all the writing materials a man would ever need, even if he were the most literate sheriff in the south west.

There was a knock on the door, and Carter, who had settled down at his fancy desk to draw up the charges for the court, gave a grunt of annoyance. Like most of his ilk he hated paperwork, and liked to get it over as soon as possible – and there was a reason why he wanted to get these particular cases out of the way, so the interruption was doubly annoying. He looked around for his young deputy, Tom Bate, but of course the young man wasn't there because he was out on one of his patrols, which was one of the reasons why Destiny had such a low crime rate.

'Come in,' said the sheriff, before remembering that the door could not be opened from the outside. This was still frontier country in many ways, and the only way to speak to the sheriff directly was by knocking and making your presence known. It had saved him from having his head blown off a few times.

He stood up, a big, impressive man wearing a cotton shirt with a faint blue stripe beneath his red waistcoat. His gun belt lay on the other desk because he always took it off when he was engaged in paperwork – it was not the most comfortable thing to wear sitting down. It bore twin holsters and there was a gun in each, but only the right-hand Colt .45 was loaded – he had never had to fire both weapons at the same time, although he had threatened plenty of miscreants with both.

'With you right now,' said Carter in a semi-amiable fashion as he tightened the belt, and there was another knock at the door. Truth be told, since he didn't like paperwork he couldn't feel that annoyed at someone who was dragging him away on business.

'Who is it?' he asked, as he always did.

'Knott,' was the short answer in a voice he recognized.

He opened up to find an opulent citizen standing before him. It was the mayor, James Maynard Knott Esquire as it announced on his official paperwork, but who always proclaimed that he was plain Jim Knott, man of the people.

He was an older man, and it was rumoured that he had fought on the Confederate side during the Civil War some twenty years before the present time. He was a tall, thin man with pleasant, even features somewhat marred by a slightly crooked nose and a few gaps in his teeth. Having come through the war it was said that he was determined to acquire land and start his own cattle business – which he had, now being one of the biggest cattle barons in the district. On his head he wore a soft black hat with an uptilted brim like those favoured by gamblers – a comparison that was apt, because above all things Jim Knott was a gambler writ large. Across his bony chest he wore a decorative vest that incorporated silk in little flashes of light blue and green against a darker shade of blue, while his trousers were in classic light brown canvas. There was an immaculate shine to his brown boots – most men wore boots of one type or another around here – but which showed that he had ridden into town and dismounted straight on to the boardwalk – and he wore a lightly cut frock coat made of dyed black cotton, light enough for the steamy south but functional enough for light summer rain.

'Johnny boy, I need a little talk with you,' said Knott.

'Come in Jim, you're always welcome.' Carter spoke lightly because he was addressing one of his greatest patrons: Jim Knott was the man who had backed him for election.

'No can do, on my way to the town hall, but if you'd care I'd like you to take a little walk with me.'

'No trouble.' Any ordinary citizen could get the ear of John Carter and he was willing to listen to them – one of the reasons he was so popular – but few could make him give up the time to go for a walk that would take him away from his many duties. He gave a visual check of the office to make sure that he had not left anything in easy reach of the prisoners, neither of whom seemed interested in anything much, then locked the door, strode to the side of his mayor and began to walk with him along the boardwalk.

'I'll get right to the point,' said Knott. 'You arrested two of my boys last night.'

'Sure did,' said Carter amiably.

'You took on a lot there son, they're good boys really.'

'The two of them were in the Goldberry saloon and a fight broke between them over a pretty girl. Them "boys" of yours frightened her half to death, 'specially when the guns came out, and that's when Seth sent one of his staff running to get me – interrupted me in the middle of a good supper, too. They was still squaring up to each other when I arrived, and there were signs it was going to turn into a riot, 'cause the other trail boys were all set to join in. They could've caused a riot that would have wrecked the joint.'

'I see.' Jim Knott looked serious for a moment, and then his face took on a lighter expression. 'Old Seth Tatters ain't got any fire in his veins. The man has gone soft with age – why, fifteen years ago he would've collared them, flung 'em out of the door, told 'em to sling it before dusting his hands together and going back inside.'

'They disturbed the peace mightily Jim, I expect they'll get no less than twenty-eight days each, Tatters will be a witness. It's him that pressed the charges.'

'Is it?' Jim Knott thought for a little while, with an appropriately knitted brow. 'Look, how about I see Tatters and square this up with him, see that he drops the charges? The girl was no better than she should have been, if you get my implications, and Seth is just seething. He'll see sense when I have a little chat with him.'

'I don't know, Jim, it's pretty serious, they was on the verge of causing a riot, they could have wrecked the man's business.'

'"Could" is not the same as "did",' said Jim Knott amiably enough. 'Now these are two good young men, just a little foolish when they've got a drink in them,' he gave a winning smile. 'Now there's a kind of selfish angle in this. They are both hard workers. We're starting a fresh cattle drive in a couple of weeks and I sure would miss their labour.'

'I'm afraid the law is the law, they were involved in a potential riot. Events like that ain't good for a small town like this, place gets a reputation pretty quickly for somewhere anything can happen. Next thing you know we'll end up like the notorious Dodge City, with folks gunning each other down in the street.'

'Ain't going to happen,' said Jim Knott. 'The law's the

reason this town is so prosperous. All right, some of the businesses here might have had slightly shady beginnings – not mine – but these are people who've settled down, become merchants and the like, and who bring huge prosperity all round. We were both voted in to keep this here place stable and well off for all, so let's keep it that way.'

'And suppose I do let the pair of them off,' said Carter, who had been thinking the matter over, 'what happens if next Saturday they come into town and start fighting all over? I'll be left with more egg on my face than I can wipe off with a good-sized bandanna.'

'That wouldn't happen,' said Knott. 'They live in one of the bunkhouses on my spread. The rest of the boys are pretty mad at them for bringing the JK ranch into disrepute. They'll be quite happy to see that they don't go out that night, and I'll enforce a curfew on 'em.'

'All right, I'll let them go if you can square it with Tatters.'

Carter meant what he said, so less than an hour later, having received the message from the owner and keeper of the Goldberry himself, he unlocked one of the cells and let out Jonas Burrows, then gave him a short lecture about not wanting to see him in town for a long time. He let Burrows go, waited for a short while, and then did the same with Lambert, who cut him short.

'I already heard the lecture, Sheriff, and sure I'm sorry, and it won't happen again,' but Carter did not like the faintly sneering expression the man wore as he strode along the porch on the outside of the office. In the near distance, waiting patiently, stood a man holding the reins of two horses. Carter recognized him as the keeper of the livery, who had obviously been primed about the release of the two men. They took the reins of their respective steeds and rode off in the direction of the JK ranch, enemies no longer but each with a sort of sullen resentment in their attitude that argued neither knew how lucky he had been.

'You should never have let them go,' said a lighter voice at his side. Carter turned and found he was facing his deputy, Tom Bate. Tom's long brown riding boots were dusty from his patrol, he wore a long brown coat made of soft wool because it had been cold that morning, the star that he wore as a proud badge of his office was pinned to a dark blue bib shirt, while his hat was of soft brown felt with a curved brim, pushed low down on his head. He had arrived just as the prisoners were being released, one hand on the Colt Peacemaker in the chocolate brown holster that he wore on his gunbelt of the same colour.

'There's a lot of reasons for letting 'em go,' said Carter, 'most of which have to do with the fact that they'll disappear soon enough with their work and won't bother this town again for a long time – if ever. I know what a taskmaster Jim Knott is. Those two will never trouble us again.'

'But there's someone who will,' said Tom.

'Who would that be? Hogan? Or his men?' (Hogan had been the other strong candidate for mayor.)

'We met at the coach station earlier,' said Tom, squinting along the road, 'and if I'm not mistaken, here she comes right now.'

11

CHAPTER TWO

John Carter was not a man who was easily surprised, he had seen too much in his two terms in office in the town of Destiny for that particular emotion to gnaw at him, so he was not perturbed by the sight that met his eyes. He saw a young woman walking along the dusty road carrying a green paper parasol against the heat of the day. On her fashionable hat was a small crown of parrot feathers, bright green and yellow, while the blue cloth of the hat was further decorated with a red band around the crown. She wore a coat cut away at the hips and beneath this an ivory blouse with ruffles that did nothing to conceal the curves of her young, swelling bosom. Her skirt was also blue, of a darker colour than her coat, and she held it up a little with her hand to prevent the hem from getting dusty from the unpaved road.

Her face was pretty and she wore little makeup – women tended not to in the hot south – but there was a firmness to her chin and a wide-open, aware look in her eyes that told Carter he was not looking at some vacuous southern debutante.

'Ah, Sheriff Carter,' she said, 'I met your deputy Tom a

little earlier. I saw him as I was coming off the train. I have been busy arranging some accommodation at the Grand Hotel on Southern Street.' By this time she had climbed the two steps to the porch and stood facing him. He could smell her flowery perfume, and he was even more acutely aware that she was a good-looking woman. Probably not as old as his first impression, because she moved and acted with a self-confidence not often found in younger females. She stuck out a hand and he instinctively shook it, feeling as if he were holding a lily flower in his leathery bear paw.

'Good morning, ma'am,' he said, doffing his hat to reveal his crown of soft, overlong black hair, 'I'm Sheriff John Carter.'

'Yes, I am well aware of your name,' she answered. 'But you won't know that I am Rebecca Seymour. Can we go inside and talk?'

'Well ma'am, it doesn't look too good if a lady, married or unmarried, comes to see me alone.'

'That may well be the case,' she said coolly, 'but nonetheless we have business to discuss, and it would be better not to air such things in public. Your deputy can act as our chaperone if that is your main concern.'

'Very well ma'am, though it is not my reputation that is a worry.'

Truth to tell, the interior of the building was a welcome refuge after the rising heat of the day. Luckily the sheriff had a coat stand for taking care of his own garments, and as she shrugged off her jacket and put her hat atop this, he was forced to extend some hospitality towards this fragrant, unexpected visitor.

'I have some coffee not long made. There's not a lot of

food around here, but I can send out for some.'

'You're fine, Sheriff, I have a feeling that most of the drink dispensed in here is water, and most of the food is bread and cheese for your – ah – involuntary occupants.' She was looking straight at the cells as she said this. He was suddenly aware of how shabby the room was, how dust lurked in every corner, how faded the paintwork seemed, how grimy the windows.

'You have not explained why you are here, Miss or Mrs Seymour.'

'That is precisely why I need to have a discussion behind closed doors,' she looked at Tom as well, the latter having said nothing since her arrival. 'Can you vouch for the probity of your deputy?'

'Wait a minute,' said Tom, understandably indignant.

'It's all right, Tom,' said Carter indulgently, 'the lady obviously has a bee in her bonnet and she needs to let it out to buzz off. How can we help you, little lady?' He smiled with the easy charm that had set plenty of hearts in town aflutter.

'Sheriff, you are a patronizing, somewhat elephantine backwater representative of the law,' she said, but not in a particularly heated manner. He felt like an insect that had just been pinned to a board. 'I am a representative of one of the best law agencies in the United States of America. I work, in other words, for Pinkerton's, and I am here to see you because I need your cooperation.' At these words he straightened up. Pinkerton's had a reputation for being one of the most stringent, thorough detective agencies in the world, let alone in America, and he was aware that their operatives were intelligent and thoroughly trained for their tasks.

14

He realized at the same time that he might have mis-judged the good-looking but firm young lady standing so tall in front of him. She was holding a leather handbag that looked capacious enough to carry not just her purse and other accessories, but also one of the small pistols that such agents carried as a matter of course.

'Well, ma'am.'

'You can call me Rebecca,' said the agent, but in a cool manner that implied they would be working together, but not intimately, 'since we'll be seeing each other quite a lot in the near future.'

'I fail to understand why that would be the case – Rebecca,' said Carter adding her name as if it was an after-thought. He was now bristling a little at her intrusion into his professional life, because he could not imagine the involvement of such an agency to be for anything except catching criminals. 'We catch our own miscreants around here,' he added, keeping his tone cool.

'Is that what you think this is about?' she asked, her manner suddenly sharp and professional – not that she had been particularly warm and friendly so far.

'Isn't it?'

'So what is going on around here that is so criminal that you want me to get involved?'

The question was like tying a knot inside his brain. He suddenly realized that he was being led down a path he did not want to explore, given that it might lead to revela-tions that he did not want brought into the light of day. It was not that he had anything to hide, he thought, not really, but he had a lot of local knowledge, and some of it might not reflect well on some of his patrons, who were also his friends.

'Say, this is just going round in circles,' said Tom Bate, good honest Tom who saw things in black and white with his youthful eyes, and who was closer in age to the young, rather bold woman in front of them. 'Just state your business now, Miss Rebecca, we ain't got all day for your fancy wordplay.'

'Tom, I do believe you have it right. I'm here to look into sephology,' said Rebecca plainly, except both men looked more baffled that ever.

'Seth who?' asked Tom, thinking it was someone's name, while Carter was a bit more canny.

'I've heard the word before,' he said, 'but it sure isn't one that's used much around these parts, so perhaps you'd better unpick it for us, miss.'

'Sephology is a little thing called voting behaviour,' said Rebecca. 'To state my needs plainly as your deputy seems to require, I've been sent to look into the last elections in this County.'

'Seems an odd thing to do,' said Carter, 'the elections were held, the mayor won, and that's all there is to it.'

'You would think so, wouldn't you, yet here I am.' Carter looked at the young woman thoughtfully.

'Well, Miss Seymour, I guess you can just go back to you hotel, pack your fancy duds and get out of here. There ain't a thing to tell, so you're wasting your time.'

'Really, and suppose I don't want to go?'

'I've never had to fling a woman out of this office,' said Carter, without any heat in his voice, and indeed with a touch of amusement, 'but me an' Tom here, well, we've hustled in here some of the biggest, meanest violent offenders you could care to name, so I guess we wouldn't have much trouble getting you to leave.' Instead of

16

responding to his not-so-veiled threats, Rebecca walked over to the teak desk that looked so out of place in these rather dingy surroundings. She sat down in the bow chair and ran her hands across the woodwork.

'My, this is a work of art. Does it belong to you personally, Sheriff? You must have paid a lot of money for this, Carter, or was it a kind of gift from some grateful patrons?'

'Why, this is the sheriff's property,' said Tom hotly, 'it's none of your business.' Carter silenced his assistant with a glare. Tom wasn't doing him any favours.

'You can do all the investigating you want, Miss, but neither of us will be cooperating with you. Now I'll ask you again to leave, because you're wasting our time. However, if you want to meet socially later on, I'll buy you a meal in a local restaurant, and we can talk off the record.'

'Is that so?' The young woman stood up, put on her coat and carefully put her hat atop her chestnut curls. 'It's just a pity that you're going to be too swamped to treat me to a meal.'

'What in the name of – in the name of the devil do you mean by that?' He had only just stopped from swearing in the presence of a woman. She was truly infuriating.

'Oh, I have to leave now, as you have requested. It's just that my letter of authority states that I must have your full cooperation.'

'What letter of authority?'

'Why, from your state governor. A delightful man. He is well aware that there have been serious moves against state corruption in Washington in the past few years. Destiny is the largest town on the Southwest Trail, and a key trading route for the area. If there has been electoral fraud in this district it could mean a lot of money for the people in

17

power. Not just because they control taxes, but due to the land grabs and deals that could take place.'

'I would have to see such a letter.' The girl was standing beside the door now, poised as if to take off. Carter knew that her implied threat was one of manpower. If he threw her out now she would muster the powers-that-be on state level to provide her with US marshals, who would come in and carry out the investigation over his head.

'Certainly,' she rummaged in her bag and brought out an ivory-coloured envelope. He recognized the state seal on the outside – a resting eagle – stamped in red wax. She opened the envelope, withdrew its contents and handed it straight to him. He read the statement on the letter and became acutely aware that his knees were exhibiting an uncharacteristic degree of weakness, while the blood was pounding like soft hammer thuds in his ears.

The statement was a short and sharp one that ordered the forces of law and order in the district to cooperate fully with the Pinkerton agent. Dully he began handing it back to her, but Tom snatched it from him and began to read it with questioning eyes.

'How do we know this is genuine? She could have had this faked.' Rebecca gave a rather attractive little shrug. Once more Carter was acutely aware both of how good looking she was and how much he wanted to be rid of her.

'Now Sheriff Carter, can we get down to business?'

CHAPTER THREE

John Carter patrolled the town of Destiny with his deputy. The town was far from large compared with those in the east, but it was big enough, and it had all the usual features of a prosperous settlement on the south-west trail. There were several saloons besides the largest and best in the form of The Goldberry. The town had no fewer than three churches – Carter was good friends with the preachers in all three – and there was the usual mix of grocery and hardware stores along Southern Street, the main thoroughfare. The streets were far from paved with gold, but they were wide and supported a huge cattle drive now and then – prosperity on the hoof.

Tom Bate had a thoughtful look on his smooth features as he looked at the sheriff. 'What are you going to do about Miss Seymour?'

'If I could, I would send her packing on the next train,' said Carter with an uncharacteristic sharpness in his tone, 'but I guess at the moment I have to give her what she wants.'

'It looks to me as if there isn't much to give her, she just wants to talk and look at a few bits of paper. That don't seem much of a problem to me.'

'Tom, don't you understand? In the end it's bits of paper that cause all the trouble in the world. Look at that letter she produced, it's a magnet for bother right there.'

'I'll go out and get some grub and be back later,' said Tom. 'Nothing's brewing, so you'll be OK until I return.' The young man did not even bother fetching his roan, but headed off to his home, which was handily in reach further down the road, where his wife Beth would have prepared him a mid-day meal of stew and potatoes.

Carter had more or less prepared his own meals and carried out his own domestic duties since his wife Linda had died a few years before. He envied this domestic bliss. He was not naturally drawn to gambling and drinking to excess, although some nights he resorted to the bottle to shut out the memories and to try and get a decent night's sleep. He still missed Linda, who had perished from an unspecified illness to do with the female condition, and although he could have had several relationships over the past few years, he had buried himself in his work. It was not that he disliked women – far from it – but he had been with Linda since he was younger than Tom Bate, and there was always a thought in the back of his mind that even if his wife was long since dead, by going with another woman he was being disloyal to her. Rebecca Seymour, for instance, now there was an example of young woman-hood, modern and forthright. He could have liked her a lot if she hadn't represented so much potential trouble.

Jim Knott was coming along the main boardwalk. By this time it was early afternoon and the sun had retained its earlier promise, making the day hot and a little muggy as it was prone to do in these parts. Carter gave his usual friendly, welcoming smile, but the mayor did not return the smile, in fact he was looking grave, like a man who had discovered that his substantial investments were worth practically nothing.

'John, I need to speak to you, sir.'

'Certainly, why not come back to the office? I can even offer you a drop of scotch.'

'No thanks.' It was not seen as a sin to drink during the day – in fact most social and even work occasions were enlivened by a small libation, but Knott was clearly not in the mood for exchanging such social graces.

'John, I was always a man of action, kept on the move. So let's do this at a trot, and get it sorted out now. First, before I look into this matter of the investigator, I want to thank you for sorting out Burrows and Lambert this morning. You won't be seeing those fellers for a long time – if ever. They might just decide to stay in Kansas after this next cattle drive.'

'How are things between you and Hogan?' asked Carter, already knowing what the answer would be, but trying to stay the inevitable query, 'and thanks for the compliment.'

They both knew Marty Hogan was his neighbouring rancher, another big shot in the area, and a man who had always taken the opportunity of bad-mouthing Knott to the sheriff, and although there was an element of humour in his put-downs, with a sense of some sort of respect for business acumen, Knott and Hogan were rivals in a cutthroat business. Maybe he was wrong, but Carter could never see how they could be real friends.

'Well, you deserve it. You do a lot to keep the peace. Hogan's still a hell-hound I would see dog-whipped down the road.' He said this with a trace of humour in his tone. By this time the two men were halfway down the main street and nearing the area where the boardwalk turned up a side street and then ran out after about a hundred feet. The street thus revealed was lined with more commercial buildings and the dwellings of the more prosperous citizens. Knott seemed more at ease now that they were away from the main traffic of the town, with less chance of being observed.

'Let's get plain and straight on this one. I don't like the snoop being around here. Where is she, by the way?'

'She's back at her hotel, she just came to see me as a courtesy, and also because she says she'll need me to accompany her to where she's going.'

'And where would that be, young John?' asked Knott with attempted lightness.

'To see you, I guess, and ask a few questions.'

'And what is this young jade going to ask? Did you cheat the election so you could get put up there and exploit the voters?'

'I never cheated anybody, Jim, but your nomination was what swung it for me. So I helped you out when I could on polling day, helped keep a watch on any trouble that might have ensued, and made sure that people got to file their ballots as they should.'

'You kept my men in order too, the hotheads – some could have caused real trouble for me that could have lost me the election, let alone that bunch sent over by Hogan.' There was a trace of quiet triumph in his voice. Hogan had been the other strong candidate for mayor, and the two men had faced off against each other several times. Each had an entourage of their own men – and women too, the wives of the voters – and it was only by recruiting several deputies and keeping regular patrols at election time that Carter had been able to keep good order.

One of his best innovations during that time had been the stripping of firearms from the supporters of each side. He had labelled these weapons, hanging them in his office, so that the respective owners could come and get them when they were about to leave town. It was a move that had saved at least ten lives by his estimate, even though some had seen it as a draconian measure against their liberty. When Hogan and the other candidates lost the election, Hogan had called for a public enquiry into vote rigging, but no one had taken him seriously and he had slipped into the background of everyday life, still feuding at a low level with the man who had defeated him at the polls and who was his rival in the cattle business.

'Sour grapes ain't pretty,' said Jim Knott, thinking of that time, 'but it's why we got to watch our backs, and I'll look after yours if you look after mine. I didn't commit a wrongdoing, but if this girl of yours stirs up enough trouble they might say there's no smoke without fire and try to bring me down.'

'What do you want me to do, Jim?'

'I want you to cling to her the way a limpet clings to a rock. Make sure you and that doofus deputy of yours track her like she was a maverick stray and bring her to heel like a bad dog. You hear me? And I want you to report it all back to me.'

'Jim, when I took on this task you said it was because I had some backbone. Well, I ain't a bought man. I'll do my job, but for the citizens of the town, not because of what you tell me to do.'

'Can't say fairer than that, it's what you gotta say, but I think we have an understanding.' By this time they were at the end of the boardwalk. The two men parted at that point, and Carter walked slowly back towards his office.

Inside him he could feel the first traces of a nagging doubt, one that grew steadily as he walked onwards. He had been friends with both ranchers before his election as sheriff, and he had always found Hogan to be a big, pleasant, approachable man. That there was a bitter rivalry between him and Jim Knott was beyond dispute, but was it entirely one-sided?

Also inside him was a growing resolve that he really was going to be his own man, whatever the mayor might think, and he was going to accompany the young woman all right, but more for her own safety than any other reason. Jim Knott had been his patron, had done a lot for him, but Carter decided at that moment that he had to be his own man, and that he had to work for the law of the land or what was the point of doing his job?

A now familiar figure came towards him, and he nodded to the girl and smiled pleasantly. She came forwards, and for a moment he felt like linking arms with her. She really was very pretty.

'Time for food, then work,' she said. They moved off together.

CHAPTER FOUR

Since it was mid-day he availed himself of the opportunity she had given to go for a meal with her. Those who knew Carter were astonished to see him with a young, attractive woman. Even Herb, who ran the local eatery, and counted Carter as one of his best customers since the death of the latter gentleman's wife, was suffering from the urge to say something as he cooked up their meal of good home fare – cooked ham, potatoes and beans. They sat at a table on seats that had seen better days, and their surroundings were somewhat dingy because Herb was not one to spend his profits on fripperies, but there was a wonderful smell of cooked food in the air, and that was enough as far as Carter was concerned.

'I have to let you know, Mr Carter, that I don't want to be known as a Pinkerton investigator,' said Rebecca. 'I saw you talking to Mayor Knott a short while ago – did you avail yourself of the opportunity to divest yourself of this information?'

'Well, they know you're an investigator of some kind. But you're safe. I gave very little away to the mayor, given he's part of your investigation. I'll say that you've been

25

sent by the state election board, which isn't so far from the truth.'

'That's good. Now I'm going to visit a number of people, and I'm going to ask them what they think of the election results. As a local man you can help by introducing me to the one person who can talk about what really happened.'

'Who would that be?'

'I believe it's Mr Hogan I'm seeking.'

'I don't think old Marty will have much to say.'

'Why would that be?'

'Let's just say he wasn't happy with the results, didn't think they were fair, which begs the question, ma'am, that you might be walking into the company of someone who's mighty biased about the whole affair.'

'I still want to see him. I'll learn as much from what he doesn't say as from what he does.' They were silent after that, except for the sounds of eating, because Herb brought their plates that were filled to the brim with good solid food, which they washed down with several coffees. Carter was surprised to see her almost match his own appetite, a prodigious feat for such an attractive woman, some of whom only picked at their food. It was a trait that endeared her to him. Was she wearing scent? And surely she had rouged her lips since he had last seen her?

'What are you staring at?' she asked with a shred of her old belligerent manner.

'Nothing,' he answered, 'nothing in particular.'

When they finished it was time to go back to business. He was going to pay for the meal, but she insisted on paying for her own share, and even gave Herb a tip. Herb, a big taciturn man who had once been a trail cook before settling down in town, was evidently struck by this exotic presence and said nothing, but there was a look on his face as the two walked out together that made Carter want to say 'What?'

She was obviously a woman who was not going to waste time, and she immediately asked Carter to help her acquire a horse. Her business would involve a great deal of riding around, because there was a lot of area for her to cover.

They went together to the livery. She was fussy enough to linger about the Hardimans, the name of the place, and study the horses. Finally she picked a young, somewhat spirited mare called Lightfoot. Carter immediately had serious doubts about her ability to handle such an animal, but as she led the horse out she quickly disabused him of this opinion.

'I'm a local girl, I come from the next county, and I have kin around these parts, I could almost ride before I could walk.'

'Now, I suppose, we'll go see the mayor?'

'I hardly think so. He's the last person we want to approach. The man we want to get to know is his main rival, Mister Hogan, and you're going to take me there first.'

Marty Hogan was not in a good mood. It had taken Carter and Rebecca at least half an hour to find him even after they arrived at the ranch, because he was performing a task every good owner should be doing in the weeks leading up to the cattle drive: he was out with his men taking an inventory of his stock. They managed to track him down to one of his barns on the outskirts of his huge ranch, where he was deep in conversation with one of his overseers. Both men were big and raw-boned, and whoever saw them for the first time would have been hard pressed to tell the owner from the employee if it had not been for the wide disparity in age. Hogan had never been able to have children with his wife Renée, but it was rumoured that some of his dalliances far off in time had provided him with offspring, and this worker was perhaps proof of this.

Hogan wore the kind of clothes that suited the wide spaces where the cattle were kept. His lower parts were clad in sturdy grey canvas trousers, much stained from the inevitable stresses of working about the ranch. He wore a striped shirt, and his trousers were held up by braces instead of a belt. He wore a gun at his hip, in a strapped-on holster, and he wore a coat of dark cotton, while his battered, wide-brimmed hat was shoved low down on his head. He did not look in the least like the tubbed and scrubbed, best suited popular candidate who had taken on Jim Knott the previous fall.

The new arrivals dismounted and walked their horses towards him.

'Mr Hogan, can we have a word with you?' asked Carter. 'Alone, if you please.'

'He ain't got the right,' protested the other man, big and young, dressed in a similar fashion to his boss.

'It's all right Elias,' said Hogan. 'You get on with your planning, and I'll deal with these two.'

'All right,' Elias went off towards where his horse was hitched to a rail at the side of the barn, but he looked back once or twice at the new arrivals as he did so.

'Haven't seen you in town much, Marty,' said Carter, as

he looked at the man whom he considered a friend.

'Don't have much to go to town for,' said Hogan. 'Not as if I was the mayor or anything.' It was obviously a topic that preyed on his mind a great deal.

'That's what this is about,' said Carter. 'This young lady here, she's kind of an investigator dealing in particular with voting behaviour.' He made his introductions and Rebecca shook hands with the cattle baron.

'I'm an election adviser,' she said, neglecting to mention the Pinkerton connection. As always, Carter wanted to let his friend know what was happening, but he bit his tongue, obeying her wishes.

'Well, young lady, you sure are a pretty addition to that perfession,' said Hogan. 'I would offer you a bite to eat up at the ranch, but I'm out here fer the day.'

'Perhaps we could meet at another time, if that suits you,' she said. There was a twinkle in his eye which said that despite his age, he was not unaware of good-looking young women.

'Well, that would be fine, but time is passing fast and we have a lot of work to do sorting out the stock and seeing what mavericks that thieving bas . . . I mean thieving swine Knott has gained from us this time.'

'Well, maybe you can do me a favour and let me know about the election?'

'What do you want to know?'

'Well, what was the conduct of the mayor both before and after the election? For instance, I hear that he flooded the town with his men. This, of course, is a serious accusation, but did you see any evidence of coercion, or feel there was any vote rigging?' Rebecca had with her a notebook and a pencil, the quickest way to take down any information that she might gain from the big rancher.

Hogan's face twisted, but instead of the stream of invective that Carter was expecting, the rancher's rugged features took on a guarded expression.

'What's this all about?'

'I have explained already,' said Rebecca failing to conceal a trace of asperity in her tone – not a good way to go with a tough rancher.

'You came all this way just to ask me that kind of question?' he asked, but did not wait for an answer. 'Let me tell you, lady, Jim Knott was a prime candidate, just like I was. The town needed a tough administration; things had been going to hell in a handcart for too long, we knew what had to be done.'

'What are you trying to say?'

'I'm saying that if you're going to be throwing around allegations of vote fixing you better be mighty careful of what you say.'

'I'm just looking at the facts, Mr Hogan. If nothing is wrong, then there's nothing to worry about. I'm just going around asking a few questions on behalf of the state.'

'Can't really say I have anything to tell you about the election. We're where we are, and that's it. I wouldn't go as far as to say the best man won, but Knott's where he is and I'm where I am. In some ways I don't envy the man, he's got a cattle drive to prepare too, along with running a town, must be a lot of work.' Hogan stared into the middle distance and it was obvious that he was not going to talk much longer, his mind being on the rounding up and branding that had to be done.

'Mr Hogan, you haven't answered a thing.'

'I really think you should cooperate with Miss Seymour, Marty,' said Carter, intervening for the first time. 'It's a serious accusation, and one that we need to look into.'

'It's "we" now, is it?' Hogan had the most penetrating blue eyes that Carter had ever seen, and he turned these on the luckless sheriff – and Carter suddenly saw the ruthless businessman beneath the amiable surface of the older man. 'I don't think I've ever said this to you, John-boy, but I give you and your purty companion ten minutes to get off my land.'

'There's a potential criminal offence here,' snapped Rebecca, suddenly showing one of the true sides to her character. 'Do you really want to be involved in something like that? I just want to ask you a few questions.'

'Ten minutes,' said Hogan, starting to walk away, 'then a few of my men'll come and make sure you leave.' He went to the side of the barn where he, too, had hitched his horse, undid the reins from a wooden rail, and began to climb into the saddle.

'Why, you. . . .' Rebecca started forward, only to find that a strong hand was restraining her by the arm. 'Let me go!'

'This is his land, and I promise you he'll keep his word, so come on, let's go.'

It had taken them quite a time to track down Hogan, so it was later in the day when they arrived in Destiny. Carter could see that the young woman, despite her youthful zest, was beginning to tire. She had been travelling all day, one way or another.

'Time for you to settle down for the day,' said Carter. 'I presume they gave you time to investigate.'

31

'They gave me a couple of weeks,' she said. By this time they were standing in his office, and he, too, was feeling tired. He would need to get some shut-eye and freshen up for the evening. The thing was, a job like this, even with a deputy and the power to swear in townspeople if trouble arose, was a twenty-four-hour business. Even if he was asleep he could be woken at any time to investigate a disturbance or deal with a theft or a shooting.

'So I guess I'll settle down for the day, but first I'll need a note of those townspeople who might have something to tell me about the rigging of the election.'

'The *alleged* rigging,' said Carter. 'We just don't know yet.'

'That's true,' she stood up and looked at him with those fine green-grey eyes that were as penetrating in their own way as Hogan's. 'Can you tell me precisely what happened out there today?'

'You want my true feelings?'

'Of course.'

'Then I think Marty Hogan knows a lot more than he's admitting.'

'But why is he being so obstructive?'

'That's the question, and I'm as surprised as you are – after the way he reacted during the elections I would have thought he would have been quite happy to storm and even rage about the shortcomings of Jim Knott, but instead he scuttled off like a frightened pup with its tail between its legs.'

'But what's he frightened of?'

'I can hazard a guess, Miss Seymour, but ultimately I think he's scared of you.'

'Scared of *me*?' the young woman was not really asking

a question of Carter, she was speaking aloud, mulling the words over in her own mind. 'Then that tells me all I need to know. I'll see you soon, Mr Carter. This is just the beginning.'

CHAPTER FIVE

Sheriff Carter hardly had time to eat and get some more refreshment before there was a new development. Tom had called in briefly, then had left to go to his kith and kin, leaving his boss in charge. This was only fair because the boss was paid a great deal more than his deputy and so had more responsibility.

The trouble was with that woman, as he was now thinking of Rebecca, she was like a worm in the centre of an apple and she would gnaw away at the fruit until she broke through the skin. In addition to this, he now reflected, there was the fact that he had not been entirely honest with her – or with himself, for that matter. There had been times when he had supported Knott, and Hogan, in the setting up of local businesses, had even helped them to obstruct those they did not want. At the time he had justified it in his own mind by saying that someone had to get the business.

But look where it had led. He strongly suspected that Seth Tatters was running a house of ill-repute above his saloon. That was all very well, but it was illegal in this county. He also suspected that Seth was watering his beer, a much more serious crime in the eyes of some.

Then he had known about the deals made by local businesses with the land companies, who had so quickly and thoroughly made huge profits from those who wanted to sell.

His train of thought was interrupted by a sharp knock at the door. Since it was evening he got out of his seat and strapped on his guns before answering. He was almost disappointed to see that it was yet another rancher, Old Man Tulloch, who had sworn that he was going to stay on his land until the day he died. He was not that old really, being in his late sixties and not much more advanced in years than his fellow rancher Hogan. But instead of being clean shaven he wore a white beard of biblical proportions and was dressed in a dusty coverall supported by shoulder straps. The coverall had once been blue but was now a bluish grey, and had not been washed in a long time. The top of his head was bald and surrounded by a cloud of fluffy white hair. All of this made him look much older than his years and like some minor prophet, while his first name added to the analogy.

'Why, it's Ezekial Tulloch,' said Carter glad of the opportunity to get some respite from his own thoughts. 'How can I help you, Zeke?'

'I need to talk, Sheriff.'

'Well, that's what I'm here for.'

'You got to help me, Sheriff. My last ranch hand took off yesterday. They won't work for me any more and my business, what's left of it, is startin' to hurt real bad.'

'Sorry, Zeke, I don't understand what this has to do with me.'

' 'Tis crimes, Sheriff, that's why. I'm being targeted to

drive me off my land.'

'And who is doing this?'

The older man looked at Carter with the red-rimmed eyes of someone who had not slept a great deal lately.

'You know fine who it is, Sheriff. I want you to see Knott and Hogan and warn them not to set their men to come into my land, or steal and kill my cattle any more. Truth is, my ranch is set squarely between theirs. They have to pay me to use my wells, they need to drive their cattle across with my permission. I charge 'em, a man has to live, and my own herds are almost down to nothing. They would be so grateful if I was out of the way. They would wait for that new land law to kick in once I was gone and claim my ranch between them. There's one girl left, a niece but she's long gone with no contact details, and we ain't in touch. I doubt of she would hear when I pass.' Carter knew exactly what law Ezekial Tulloch was talking about: if land became fallow for six months or more, unless claimed by a relative – and Tulloch had just one who was never in touch, it seemed – then the other local landowners could put in a deposition to have the land divided between them.

'Sorry about this, Zeke, but there's not much I can do. Have either of the ranchers in question ever threatened you openly?'

'No, I guess not. It's what they do with their men, that's the problem, they ain't exactly going to do it in person, are they?'

'So who's being causing the trouble?'

'Masked men, coming in, stealing my cattle, killing them, making fires on my land so the feed gets burned.'

'Zeke, that's still no proof of who's doing this, and you know it.'

'So you'll do nothing for me?'

'The other thing is, I was appointed as the town sheriff, and anything that happens in the ranches short of murder is really outside my jurisdiction.'

'Sheriff, this will be a murder case if you don't help me.' Carter looked at the old man and said something that he would later regret:

'Look, I know you've been offered a buy-out for the Lazy Z from one or other of the barons. I would advise you to take the money and go, Zeke.'

'So you ain't going to help me then, Sheriff? One law for them and another for me, is that it? It's well known you're in their pockets. Why, you can't even help law-abiding citizens when they're being abused.'

'What did you say?' Carter's expression had hardened, and he no longer looked the popular sheriff elected by a huge majority. 'I'm my own man, Zeke, no one buys me.' For a second he looked insulted enough to reach for his gun, a practice not unknown in these parts when citizens felt they had been dishonoured in some way. Then he relaxed his glare and gave a brisk shake of his head as if throwing off some kind of weight. 'All right Zeke, I'll send out Tom to have a look at what's going on. Just give me some facts and figures.'

And Zeke did.

Tom Bate rode out towards the Lazy Z ranch with little on his mind. The ranch was a surprising distance out of town. Many people thought of Kansas as being a place of wide open country, and indeed it was in certain places. But in the south-west region the plains were no longer so wide open, the huge tracts of land to be found there had long ago been annexed by the profitable cattle business. He could understand why the two cattle barons needed to access this area, because it was situated squarely between the M Bar H and the JK ranches. He could even see the branding irons that represented those particular parties in his mind.

It was a fine day, too, as he set out over the green land of the plains. Because this area was not as intensively farmed for feed as the other two, there was more greenery and many clumps of cottonwood trees, most of which would have been felled on the land of the other ranches.

He was not at all troubled by the issues laid out before him that morning by Sheriff Carter. After all, a few reprobates might try and scare an old man, but they could hardly do much to a fully armed representative of the law.

He was met by the old man himself. Zeke was on a horse that had traces of grey on its muzzle, indicating that it was an old favourite.

'I'm goin' to take you to where they most commonly do their damage,' said Zeke. He was not a man who talked a lot, and he seemed to think that this was enough information. However, Tom was not one to shirk his duties as they were laid out before him.

'I need to know exactly what's been happening.'

'The blunt truth is, they come on to my land. They kill my cattle and destroy my property. They just won't leave me alone.' His expression took on a trace of bitterness. 'Now the last of my men have left. I can't blame old Pete, it looks like the end.' It was in Tom's mind to ask him why he didn't sell out and move on, but he suppressed the question, which was answered a moment later by an outburst from Zeke.

'They think they can make me sell! I'll settle fer one thing. I'll go down in a blaze of glory, shooting. I didn't fight in the Civil War for my freedoms, for this very state, just to let some young idjits come in and take over.'

'I see,' Tom nodded, thinking that if his situation was this desperate he would just cave in and go. After all, it wasn't as if the old man didn't have any other options. But then a thought occurred to him, what if someone was trying to drive him, Tom, and his wife Beth out of their home, was that something he would put up with or would he fight back? The answer was clear, resting in his mind. Without another word they rode off together.

On any ranch there had to be outbuildings for feed storage. It wasn't long before they came to one of these, it was really just a big, clapboard shed with a pent roof that sloped down on one side. The reason it wasn't flat was that the torrential rains that swept in from the mountains would, at their heaviest, cave in a level roof.

'I need to show you something.' They got off their horses and hitched them to a scarred wooden rail on the side of the building. The shed had once been painted green, but many years of wind and weather had reduced the colour to a faded grey. 'Come on here, this is what you need to see, boy.' They had approached the shed from behind because of the way it sat on the plain, and now they went round to the entrance – and Tom gave a low whistle at what he saw. The front of the building was blackened and blistered where it had evidently been licked by flames.

'When did this happen?'

'Oh, just a few days ago.'

'How come it didn't burn down?'

'These clapboard sheds, they get filled with damp

during the rainy season and it's hard to get a flame to take on a flat wall when you just throw down lit torches and ride off. It's getting worse, they're breaking the law, not just harassing me, but destroying my property. I need you and Sheriff Carter to do what's right by me.' There was a look on Zeke's face that Tom did not like, one of defiance, mixed with another emotion that at first the young man did not recognize – then he realized it was fear.

Zeke Tulloch was scared to death.

That was when they heard the noise. Horses have a distinctive rolling sound to their hoofs as they thunder across the plains, quite unlike that of the cattle that Tom had already seen ambling around on the grass picking up feed here and there. It was evident that they were going to get some company, perhaps from the very people they did not want.

'Get into the shed,' ordered the young deputy.

'I don't want to do that.'

'Just do as I say.' Tom practically pushed the old man into the storage building. There was a smell of preserved winter feed mixed with acrid traces of smoke as he shoved Zeke in. Tom turned and ran to where he had heard the sound of horses. Three men were riding by, all of them carrying burning wooden torches, the smell of pitch and turpentine telling the lawman what they had used to light them. They were all wearing their hats low over their heads, and red and white spotted bandannas around their faces. All three were whooping and yelling as they rode swiftly on. Almost in unison they threw their torches at the unburned side of the building and the flames took in the dry grass there.

Tom came running out to the entrance of the building

with a gun in either hand, but by then the torches had already been thrown, the flames were sprouting in the dry grass and the horses on which the men were perched were galloping swiftly away. Tom did what instinct told him and shot at the fast retreating men, and he had some luck because one of the intruders gave a shout of pain and slumped in the saddle. One of the others turned a pistol in hand, and shot at the luckless deputy. Luckless because the shot caught him on the side and spun him around so that he hit against the shed wall and fell down amid the flames.

In a few seconds the horsemen were gone, including their wounded companion.

CHAPTER SIX

'Well, I've never said this before,' said Carter, 'but Zeke is a hero. Without him Tom would be gone by now.' He was standing inside the home of his deputy, talking to the wife of his fellow lawman. The house was neatly appointed and well kept by the young woman who stood at his side. Beth was barely twenty years old and she had beautiful doe-like eyes, long fair hair, and was altogether a wonderful, hard-working young woman who doted fiercely on her youthful husband and gave him her unswerving loyalty. She was looking at her husband right now, because he was in their back bedroom on the flock-filled mattress atop the iron-framed bed. Right now Tom had his side bandaged and his left arm too, and he had some minor burns on his face and neck.

'Zeke dragged him away from the flames and did the right thing, he made sure he was well away from the burning building – he's a wiry old guy for his age, comes of looking after stock all his life, I guess – then he rode into town as fast as he could and alerted me as to what was going on. I got Dr French and a couple of the local guys I've used to come out with me, got Tom strapped up and brought him back real fast. The doc's given him a dose of morphine, but he'll need a bit of rest, let that bullet wound knit. Don't worry about the medical bill, he was injured on duty, I'll make sure the state picks up the tab.'

'Why did you let this happen?' Beth suddenly pulled away from the sheriff, a look of utter fury on her usually attractive features. 'You knew what was going on and you still sent him in.'

'The fact is, he was just doing his duty,' said Carter. He brooded a little over the matter. 'I guess I could've gone out with him and perhaps things would've been different, we might of got hold of one or two of those miscreants, cleared up the mystery of whose doing this to Zeke.'

'I think we all know what's happening!' she said, still furious. 'Now, Sheriff, I'd be obliged if you would get out of here right now, and don't come back. You're not welcome in our home!'

Carter jammed his hat down low on his head and marched out of the building. He had always got on well with Beth and now because of this affair he had fallen out with her in a spectacular fashion, and what was more he couldn't really blame her for how she felt. If he had taken Zeke more seriously he wouldn't be seriously lacking in manpower right now.

As he walked down the road his heart sank even more when he saw that he was facing Rebecca Seymour. She was outside his office, and the look on her face was one that showed she was not going to be put off easily. He let her into the building. Because he had been dealing with the investigation into the attack on Tom and Zeke, it was already heading towards mid-day. He was sore from riding most of the morning, and he had yet to have his second coffee of the day. He greeted her, then put the coffee on the stove to boil, asking her if she wanted some, but she refused, having taken refreshment at the hotel.

'I heard what happened to Mr Tulloch, and your deputy,' she said. 'Is Tom going to be all right?'

'I guess so,' said Carter, 'he'll need a couple of days to recover, but it was a wound to his side, so I guess it'll scar over. It'll be painful for a while, and he has a few minor burns. It's not his wounds that worry me, but whether he can take the fact that he could be attacked for nothing. I've seen good men who couldn't take it.' He drank his coffee, allowing the liquid to soothe his jangled nerves.

'So I take it you're going to do something about the attacks on Mr Tulloch now?'

'Sure, I'll get a few locals who owe me a favour and we'll do one or two patrols of his land,' said Carter.

'Patrols, what good will those do?'

'We might scare 'em off for a while if they know the law's involved.'

'Listen to you,' she put her hands on her hips and squared up to him, 'you should be investigating, finding out who those men were. One of them was wounded, he'll need treatment. You could ask around and find out who's looking after him. You know, do your job.'

'Right now, my job is to look after you while you go around finding out if the election was rigged so you can do what all snoops do and bring the bad men to heel.'

'Snoop? I have a profession, if you want to know!'

'Then you can perform your profession without me.' He began to pull on his jacket, which had been hanging on the coat stand.

'Where are you going?'

44

'To get together some men I can trust and do a patrol at Tulloch's,' he said. 'No time like the present.'

'And what about my work?'

'I guess I can't split into two. I'll see you later; do more of your useless interviews that go nowhere.' He could see that he had hit home, her eyes were sparkling, and not with pleasure but with anger.

'I will see you later, Sheriff, and this will be done. In the meantime I will make some enquiries of my own amongst the local businesses, in a discreet way. Don't tell anyone anything about me. When will you be back?'

'I don't know,' he shrugged, 'it's a long ride. You can do your investigations in the early evening I guess.'

'I suppose so,' the look on her face was hard. 'If I had my way I wouldn't want to see your smug face again.' She walked to the door, opened it, went out and slammed it behind her so that it reverberated in the door frame for a moment, the thud of her exit ringing in his ears.

He now had the dubious record of irritating two attractive women within the same hour, not something to which he would have aspired.

Resignedly he checked his guns to make sure that they were cleaned, oiled and fully loaded with bullets. Like any good lawman he always made sure his weapons were in full working order. In the past, during saloon confrontations and when holding up bank robbers his weapons had been of firing quality while theirs had jammed, a fact that had saved his life more than once. He was like a soldier going into war.

He knew that Zeke had returned to his ranch. He took a Winchester off the gun rack and made sure that that, too, was in working order, then headed towards the outside world. He would ask Bell, Curran and Atkins to join him on his expedition, good men who would back him up if there was any trouble, and all for a small reward from the state. He went out to his roan and sheathed the Winchester in its holder, then began to undo the reins of the animal where it was tethered outside the building. He was a little in shadow as he did this, a fact that probably saved his life.

Maybe it was a kind of instinct that he had developed over the years, but as he stood there, he felt a crawling sensation at the nape of his neck and moved away from the roan – just as a shot came and kicked up the dirt precisely where he had been standing – he could even smell the richness of the dirt where it had been burned by the bullet.

Instinctively he ran along the road, jumping on to the boardwalk so that he was now in shadow. This did not stop the unknown would-be assassin from shooting at him another three times, the bullets kicking at his heels and rattling the wood beneath him as he ran, until finally he came to Herb's eatery, flung himself inside and slammed the door, just as Rebecca had done a short while ago, only out of desperation not temper. He stood there in front of his friend breathing deeply.

'Coffee?' asked Herb hopefully, not being one to question anybody, even a man who had just burst into his establishment with a red face and the look of someone who had just been trying to run a mile in a few minutes.

'No thanks, later,' said Carter who was about to leave, and do some investigation of the would-be killer on his heels. As he stood there with the scent of fresh coffee temptingly filling his nostrils he mentally reviewed what had happened, now that he was not under immediate threat.

From the way the gunshots had followed him, and their impact, he knew that someone had been shooting at him from a high vantage point, and he knew the shots were coming from an increasingly wide angle as he ran. The experience had taught him one thing he had known instinctively from the moment he started running.

Someone, he didn't who or why, wanted him dead.

'That sure is a hell of thing,' said Herb, 'you coming in here like that. For a moment I thought the Sullivans was after you.'

'Why would you think that?' Carter tried to keep his tone casual.

'Well, Barney Sullivan's in town. I heard he was still pretty sore at you.'

'What's he doing here?'

'Just in for a few hardware supplies. He was in here earlier on today, him and that younger brother of his, Henry, for some grub to fortify them for the day ahead. I guess it's not every day they get a meal cooked for them by a professional.' Carter had to suppress a smile at this, despite his ordeal, because Herb cooked the most basic food like eggs and bacon on a greasy skillet.

The Sullivans were something else. They were not so much a family as a clan, and lived out even further across the boundaries of the main ranches, having a settlement of their own in an area of the south west called Pleasant Valley. In his own mind it had always been a kind of hidden rule of thumb that if an area is called Sunnyvale, or Green Street, it is usually one of the worst places in the area. This held true for Pleasant Valley, which was located beside a tributary of the Greater Missouri, and was deeply lined and scarred with rocky pinnacles, redoubts and bluffs, not great for cattle but at least with plenty of greenery and lush grass down by the water, and natural rocky corrals for keeping their cattle and horses.

'Herb, is there another way out of here?' His mind was working overtime now, and he had been given enough of a pause to come up with a makeshift plan.

'Sure, I have a side entrance on to an alley rather than a back door.'

'That'll do fine.' Herb led him through to the part of the building where he kept his stock of food supplies – boxes of eggs, and meat that had been wrapped and kept on cool shelves, and salted, preserved pork – towards a door that was a little heavier than the one at the front. Herb took a set of keys that jangled from his waist and opened the door.

'Can I ask what this is about, Sheriff?'

'Yes. Someone's been shooting at me with intent to kill,' said Carter. 'I ain't about to walk out of your front door and present a frontal target for the bastard. On the other hand, if there's some lunatic with a weapon out there I got to find out who it is because I have a duty not just to protect my own person, but the town.' This was a far different man from the one the café owner normally dealt with. There was a grim certainty on Carter's face that did not bode well for whoever had tried to splash his brains over the boardwalk.

Leaving Herb – who hastily locked the door behind him, wanting no part in this new development – Carter found that he was in an alleyway littered with scraps of decaying food, old barrels, one or two broken boxes and little else except dust. Such alleyways were seldom frequented by anyone except for owners gaining access to their businesses.

He could have made his way out to the main street from here, but something stopped him from doing so. A person who was as high up as he suspected the gunman to be would still have a superb vantage point to pick off anyone emerging from the space between the buildings.

Instead he looked backwards towards the other end of the alleyway. A feeble attempt had been made to block off the back way with a few boards nailed between the two buildings. They were too high to jump over, but one of the bottom ones was rotten, and it gave way to a swift kick from one of his solid boots. Not feeling best pleased at crawling under this, he found that he was at the back of the buildings that lined the main street and not that much further along from his own office. Behind him was a jumble of small businesses and dwelling places. Destiny had not been built to any particular plan, and rich and poor lived cheek by jowl.

This was not the first time he had been involved in a situation that might have led to his demise, and in a way he was not that worried. He knew he was capable of dealing with a would-be killer, especially now that he knew such a killer was out there.

He was not, however, in the mood to show much in the way of mercy for such a person. John Carter had one maxim in life, and that was if someone tried to shoot him, he had a right to gun that person down. The law said that he had to bring that person to justice, but to Carter's mind, personal justice and the word of the supposed rulebook were two different things.

There was still a trace of heat in the air as he walked towards the back of his own jailhouse. He had never realized how big the mostly unused cell block was – it stuck out from the back of the building and was made of solid red brick, the four cells arranged in such a way that the barred windows allowed in some light to each individual space.

There was a Chinese laundry, of all things, beside the jail, and the yard at the back of this was littered with the tools of its trade – scrubbing boards, tubs and big washing sticks, not to mention the actual laundry fixed on rope lines with big wooden pegs, the clothes fluttering in the welcome breeze. The workers, who still wore the pigtails and cut-away jackets traditional in their own land, were busy plying their trade. They liked working outdoors in good weather.

'Sheriff Carter,' said the owner, Xi Ping, looking pleased to see the lawman. 'What bring you here?'

'I need to use your space,' said the sheriff, without giving any explanation. 'I won't be long.' The owner, who was a little old man somewhat stiff in movement, wearing a kind of smock and black leggings, smiled and gave a gracious nod, as if to say 'anything to help'.

Carter gave him a nod of thanks, then swiftly made his way up the side of the laundry. He was now on the far side of his own building, in a much cleaner space than the one beside Herb's. Still in the shadows he looked towards the buildings across the road. His office was situated directly across from a hardware store ironically called 'Hardiman's'. The lower part was, of course, where commerce took place, but the upper part was where the family of the owner lived. The roof was far from steep. Building materials were expensive, so even buildings with two floors tended to be quite low. There was a corresponding space between the hardware store and its neighbour.

Literally minutes had passed since the attack upon him, but Carter knew how swiftly events could move. Crouching low so that he was less of a target he ran swiftly across the road and down the alley across the way. Even as he did so he heard what could only have been the thump of a solid body hitting the ground. By the time he rounded the corner he could not see anyone, so whoever had descended had been very much alive.

He had missed his gunman by seconds.

CHAPTER SEVEN

Rebecca Seymour was not going to allow the setbacks of the day to stop her from doing her job. Even though she was a Pinkerton agent, she was in a kind of open disguise. She decided that the best way for her to proceed was to start asking questions on her own about the election that might have been fixed by the very man who had won.

She went into the Goldberry saloon and saw that it was quite busy for the time of day. The cattle drive was due to start in a couple of weeks and extra workers would be taken on, and some of the men who hoped to be employed by the big ranches were indulging in a cowboy's favourite pastimes, namely drinking and playing cards. Many of them stopped and stared at this vision of demure good looks who had stepped amongst them. One or two of the cowboys were quite handsome, and she was not immune to such temptations, but she had a job of work to do, and it was the saloon owner who was her target.

On her way to the bar as she threaded her way past some round tables, one burly cowpoke barred her way with a sturdy arm.

'Say missy, how's about we do a little rousing together?'

'Let me pass.'

'Aw the little missy's getting upset,' said the big, drunken pig of a man, 'give us a kiss, baby!' His companions, equally coarse, were laughing heartily. It seemed that any woman who had the temerity to walk into a drinking establishment was fair game. These were the last words he said to her because she balled one of her delicate-looking hands into a fist and punched him squarely on the bicep of the arm blocking her way. He swiftly withdrew the offending limb and gave a grunt of pain while she sailed blithely on. His friends were in fits of laughter at his discomfiture.

Seth Tatters was at the bar cleaning some glasses with a damp cloth and pretending to be absorbed in his task. Just the same, he had been keeping an eye on what was happening. He was a tall man with an austere expression who wore a green shirt and cuffs that were rolled up beyond the wrists to prevent them from getting wet from foaming beer. He had dark hair plastered low over his forehead, and looked more like an undertaker than the owner of the largest saloon in the area.

'I don't serve unaccompanied women,' he said as she came to the bar, making his position clear.

'I'm not the only unaccompanied woman here,' she said, her eyes sweeping around the large floor area to where several young and not-so-young women were sitting around, some talking to men but others quite alone.

'They work here,' he said briefly. 'Now I'll bid you good-day miss, unless you're looking for a job.'

'Never mind your drink,' she said in a low voice, 'I'm here on business.'

'Yep, I guessed as much.'

'Rebecca Seymour's my name.'

'Heard about you. You're the jade from out of town that's snooping around and prying into a man's business.'

'I'm looking into the election last fall. I'll ask you straight out, you would have been involved. Do you think there were any problems with the process, and do you think there was any vote rigging?'

'Lady, I don't know about such things, all I want to do is get more business and make a profit, that's what it's all about.'

Several shots were heard outside. Rebecca turned her head. The shots did not all happen at once, but had intervals in between. Tatters listened with interest.

'Wonder what's going on there? Last shots fired were in this very place Saturday night between two drunken idjits, had to get the sheriff in, and even their aim went wide of the mark.'

Shootings were uncommon in the main town, so the event was of interest to everyone there. One or two of the men went to find out what had happened, but came back none the wiser. Tatters turned his attention to the more immediate issue.

'So, lady, it's time for you to leave, and don't hit any more of my clients on the way out.'

'What if I choose to stay?'

'Lady, these here girls will help you out.' Tatters gave a brief nod and two of the working women came forwards. It was not the done thing for a man to roughhouse a woman in any manner, but there was no rule about the fairer sex doing so. 'Help this young lady out,' said Tatters, 'and if she don't show willing, do what you need to do.'

'That won't be necessary,' said a young, tall man who

unwound himself from a table nearby. 'This young lady is with me.' He was just a little bit older than her, and was dressed in a dark waistcoat over a white shirt with a string necktie. His trousers were also white, and he wore long black riding boots. In addition there was something familiar about his face, as if she had seen a photograph of him somewhere.

'Introduce us, Seth,' said the stranger. Tatters looked as sour as a man who has just bit down on a lemon.

'Miss Seymour, this is Mr Ralph. That's the name he likes to be known by.'

'Now that the formal introductions are over, would you care to have a drink with me, Miss Seymour?'

'That sounds fine, I'll have a pink gin.' Normally she would never drink on duty, but she was feeling shaken by the events of the last few minutes, especially the gunshots. Besides, this Ralph was easy on the eye and seemed pleasant enough.

'Fine, I'll have another beer, Seth, and a pink gin for the lady.' They sat down together with their drinks.

'So do *you* know anything about the elections, Mr Ralph?' she asked as he raised a glass to salute her.

'Plenty,' he said, 'what do you want to know?' It seemed that she had struck gold in the most unexpected of ways.

Carter went back to the main street and looked around as a detective might, watching out for any unusual behaviour, but except for knots of anxious people who had been in the street when the gunshots had happened, all of whom he knew, he did not see anyone whom he thought could have made the attempt on his life.

He went to the back of the hardware store, a wooden

structure with two low floors as he had surmised, and saw that with the wooden barrels at the back and a balustrade at the window in the second floor, it was easy for some intrepid gunman to scramble up on to the gentle slope of the roof and lie in wait for anyone to come out on the opposite side of the street. He went back around and into the hardware store. The proprietor, Chas Winkleton, a man in a blue bib coverall, who wore a white shirt beneath with sleeves rolled up above his elbows, was already alert for a visit from the sheriff.

'What's all the fuss about?'

'Were you aware that someone was on your roof?' asked Carter.

'That's a surprise.'

'Well, said person was trying to plug me in the head,' said Carter, 'just thought I'd let you know.'

'Well, I sure am bamboozled by that one,' said Chas. 'I heard the shots like everyone else, 'n' it caused quite a stir.'

'There's someone with a mighty grudge against me,' said Carter, 'and on the same tack, did you get a visit today from Barney Sullivan?'

'Sully? Sure, he was here earlier today. That's right, he don't like you much, do he?'

'You could say that. When the mayor asked me to pay them a visit over their incursions into his land – Hogan's too, if it comes to it – he was in a mighty combative mood. I had to lay the law down, shoot up in the air near a couple of his boys to put the wind up 'em. They were never hit of course, but he took it pretty hard, said if I wasn't wearing a badge and it was a federal offence he would have blown my head clean off my shoulders.'

'I kinda see why he came to mind,' said Chas, 'but you

miss one thing out. Sully's in his late middle years and he's kinda built like a bear, he ain't exactly the athletic type, so he'd be more likely to come through the roof than lie on it, is my guess.'

'Say, that's probably the case.'

' 'Sides, you know what he's like, came into town and bought a huge amount of stock – seeds, feed, tools – and lit out as soon as he could. Doesn't like to be away from his own little kingdom for too long.'

'I guess so. Well, thanks Chas. At least I've given you a story for when you go drinking with your buddies.'

'I'll go out back and make sure that area's cleared, won't happen again. Sure is a turn-up for the book when even the sheriff ain't safe to go about his business!'

Carter did not say so, but as he left the building he thought the same.

There was nothing he could do but start preparing for the ride out to Zeke's spread. Whatever else happened he was not going to be deterred from what he had promised to do. The men who had wounded Tom had made a bad mistake, because by shooting him they had made their business subject to the law, and even if the area had, strictly speaking, been outside his jurisdiction before, it certainly wasn't now.

He managed to get together three of the men he wanted. All three were brimming with curiosity about who had tried to kill him, but he was taciturn on the matter, merely informing them that not everybody in town was friendly towards him, which was the understatement of the year. The fourth man he wanted was a former ranger known as 'Grizzly', who often frequented the Goldberry, so it was to this establishment that he headed. The former ranger knew the country better than anybody. It was said he had Indian blood, and that made him good at finding clues others would have missed.

He entered the saloon through the traditional batwing doors and spotted Grizzly in the corner having a quiet beer, and waved to him. Grizzly knew what it meant when the sheriff appeared, and he was always willing to alleviate the boredom of his retirement by going out on one expedition or another.

Instead of going to see his old friend, the sheriff was distracted by a sight that he would not have expected to see, even though he had let her go for the day. Rebecca was sitting with a young man whom he instantly recognized as Ralph Knott, the eldest of the mayor's sons. He felt straightaway that perhaps this was not the best situation in which she should find herself. He nodded to Grizzly, and made a gesture that the latter should stay where he was for the present time, and marched over to where the couple were sitting. Indeed they *could* have been a couple with their good looks, white teeth and easy air of sudden companionship.

'So I guess the real test of a good horseman is how well he can get his steed to jump. I've had mine leap over everything from fences to rocks – big ones – and brooks, without once falling off,' said Ralph. 'I guess I was born to be in the saddle – couldn't be helped, being brought up with all those riders. I've been roping steers, too, since the age of nine, started with calves o' course, but boy, did I work my way up.'

'That's excellent,' Rebecca was saying, 'tell me more, and I'll buy you a beer while we're talking. Now about those elections, what was it you were saying?'

'The elections, sure, the ballot boxes were all over town, some of 'em was even in here. Biggest ever election for years, a real rally, and all the beeves was forgotten about that day I can tell you, cos the good ol' boys was right here in town doing their bit to get him elected.'

'To get who elected?'

'Why, Jim Knott of course, there never was any real opposition.' Carter had been standing at an angle to the good-looking young couple – it was a busy saloon and they weren't turning their heads every time someone new came through the door. Now he came round to where they were sitting and looked at them both.

'I see you haven't been wasting any time,' he said. He looked at the glass beside her, which was still over half full. 'Drinking on the job, Missy Rebecca? Tut tut, I never would've thought that of you!'

'Go away Mr Carter,' she said coldly, 'I thought you had a job to do, with regard to protecting Mr Tulloch?'

'Maybe that's true, and maybe that's what I was up to. But this here, it don't look much like research to me.'

'You kin take your friend away as soon as you want,' said Tatters from the bar, 'and I ain't serving her, nor talking to her, neither. She's got no business to be here. 'Specially with Master Ralph.'

'Time for you to go, Mister Carter,' said Ralph and there was a faint sneer on his face that had not been visible when he was talking to the girl.

'That's *Sheriff* Carter, and well you know it,' said the lawman.

'Well, I guess you got no jurisdiction over someone having a drink,' said Ralph, 'so why don't you take yourself off now, and we'll forget all about it?'

'Did he give you his name?' asked Carter over the head of this young nemesis.

'He was kind enough to speak to me,' said Rebecca, 'Ralph and I are getting rather friendly.'

'No, that's not what I meant,' said Carter, 'did he tell you his full name?'

'Nothing secret here,' said Ralph. 'Tell the lady.'

'He's Ralph Knott, son of the mayor,' said Carter tersely. He did not add the words 'son of the very person you're investigating, part of the problem', but it was clear from the silence that followed and the look she was giving him that she understood exactly the message he was trying to convey.

'Tell you what,' said Ralph, 'you trot off and search for bad guys and I'll stay here and guard the fort. I'll do as good a job as you, Carter.'

'What's that supposed to mean?'

'It means nothing, and everything.' Ralph Knott unwound his long body from the seat on which he had been facing Rebecca.

'Ralph,' said Rebecca, but he ignored her.

'Sheriff, you just walk in here and think you can take over, but life ain't like that. So I advise you to get on your horse and take the longest amble ever.'

The two men were now facing each other in the space between the tables. Ralph had a Colt at his side in a brand-new pristine holster, and he was faintly drunk. Carter was big and solidly built, while the younger man still had the slender build of youth.

'Ralph, I'll give you one chance to stand down, and if you don't, I'll be taking you in and throwing you behind bars for threatening a representative of the law. And if you go for that gun in your fancy holster I won't be answering for the consequences.' There had been a piano playing in one corner, with groups of gamblers at various tables arguing in a good-humoured way as they drank and played cards, but now there was a silence in which you could have heard a mouse scuttle by.

'So that's it,' Ralph seemed to have come to a sudden decision. He relaxed his stance and pulled his right hand away from his gun, while the look on his face was openly mocking. 'Big man Sheriff gets his pleasures by picking on innocent citizens. There's another big man going to get to know of this. You'll get yours soon enough. As for you, lady, you want to pick better company.' Deliberately and insolently he turned his back to the lawman and strode out of the saloon in a slow, mocking manner, pausing at the batwing doors to give a last derisive wave of his right hand just before he left the building.

There was a sudden noise from behind the bar and Seth Tatters stood there caressing a lethal-looking shotgun. He laid this on the bar with a rattling sound, but kept his hands on the weapon. Everyone knew that the saloon keeper had used the weapon at least once on a customer who had been set on strangling one of his girls upstairs, and that the killing had been seen as self-defence.

'Are you threatening me?' asked Carter mildly.

'Nope, but I ain't going to have gunplay in my bar,' said Tatters. 'That goes for you just as much as anybody, Carter. Now get out and take that critter with you.' Rebecca looked as if she was going to take the barman to task for calling her a 'critter' but Carter got her by the arm, getting her to her feet.

'Out,' he said, and such was the force of his steely personality that she obeyed. Carter signalled to Grizzly to keep waiting, and went outside with the girl. She stood there outside the green and gold-painted building breathing heavily so that her ample bosom heaved in a way that Carter would have found quite alluring in other circumstances.

'You idiot,' she began.

CHAPTER EIGHT

Carter had managed to get together his four men, Curran, Atkins, Bell and Grizzly (who was also known as Bill.) The four of them discussed mainly the matter of who had been shooting at the lawman earlier in the day, and he had to confess that he did not have the slightest clue as to who might have committed the deed. After that the conversation languished somewhat as the men rode into what might be dangerous territory.

The trouble for Carter was that this gave him plenty of time to think, and he cast his mind back to his confrontation with Rebecca outside the saloon. She had striven to keep her voice low, but the flashing of her eyes and the intensity of her tone told him more than anything else.

'Did someone appoint you for your brawn rather than brains?' she asked rhetorically.

'I just thought you should know who you were talking to.'

'I went in there to get information. I see a young, spoiled man who's had a couple of beers and wants to talk to me. Don't you think I would know immediately that he was connected with one or other of the cattle barons?

Either way he would have been useful to me.'

'In what way?'

'He was young and slightly drunk and he was impressed by my looks. That's a recipe for getting information out of any man.' Carter had to admit that he had not looked at the situation from that point of view.

'What I saw was a woman who was in danger, who didn't really know what she was getting into.'

'Oh, I've met men like Ralph and Seth Tatters before, I can handle them. Don't worry about me.'

'It's my job to worry about you. There's a lot of strange things going on in this town, and right at this moment I don't feel too easy just standing here after someone tried to gun me down outside my own office.'

'What?' She looked at him with wide, shocked eyes, some of her anger fading away. He told her the brief story of the assassination attempt and she listened intently.

'It seems to me, Sheriff, that you have a lot more to worry about than I imagined. You'll have to be wary from now on, look out for whoever is doing this to you.'

'Thanks for that, I'd already worked that out in my own head.'

'So you do have some reasoning ability after all?' The words were sharp but her tone was softer. 'Oh God, I heard those shots when I was in the saloon. You could have been killed and my mission would have been in danger.'

'Thanks for the concern, lady.'

'Well, you have to investigate what's happened to Zeke – Mr Tulloch. I'll keep going around and asking a few more questions. I guess I'll have to see you later, lawman.' Her tone was friendlier now, but his next approach sparked her off again.

'You'll go back to your hotel right now and stay there until I return.'

'What?'

'There's some mad man going around taking shots at people. You could be next; I don't want to see you in any danger. Return to your hotel where you can write up your notes to the governor, and I'll accompany you where you want to go next.'

'No,' her tone was flat. 'I'm here to do a job, and it's going to get done. You can do yours,' she held her head high and marched away, showing beyond doubt that the conversation was over. He could have pursued her, grabbed and held her and tried to make her see sense, but he had been a married man, and he knew that the worst way to deal with a woman was to try and force her to listen to him. Besides, curious onlookers had gathered across the street, not to mention the inhabitants of the saloon, some of whom had drifted from the interior to the doors to listen to what was being said.

'The hell with you, woman,' said Carter in a low voice, but that part did not matter anyway because she was already around the corner. Feeling almost consumed with rage he marched in the opposite direction, before remembering that he was supposed to be recruiting helpers, so he turned to go back to the Goldberry to fetch Grizzly.

'Hey, Sheriff,' he had been so deep in his thoughts that he started when that very person spoke to him. 'How are we going to handle this?'

'We'll patrol Zeke's spread together,' he said firmly, 'and if there's any sign of these masked men we'll try and capture them, then maybe we'll be able to clear up the mystery of who is trying to drive him away. We'll try and capture them alive,' he was speaking to the rest now, and they all agreed, although he could see a gleam in the eyes of one or two of them, which said that if it came to a shoot-out they would go as far as they needed.

They did as promised, meeting up with Zeke at the ranch he had shared for so long with his wife and family, all of whom had passed, leaving only the vanished niece of all his relatives, who had vanished and was unlikely to come forward. The ranch had been built in the 1840s when Zeke was a young man, with help from his family, and was still one of the most rustic-looking buildings in the area. After a few pleasantries with the owner the men rode around the entire spread and it took a couple of hours, but short of seeing plenty of cattle and a few damaged outhouses, they found nothing.

'I wouldn't worry about it, Zeke,' said Carter. 'They'll know we've taken some kind of action. They'll leave you alone now, or they'll have the law to answer to.'

If only he believed it was true.

When they got back to town the first thing he did was to knock on the door of the house along from his office. When Beth appeared, looking a little harassed, her hair not as neat us usual, he gave her a reassuring smile.

'I know what you said earlier, but I'm concerned, I've come to see Tom.'

'I told you, Sheriff . . .' she began, a mulish look on her young face that indicated she was not going to allow him entry, when there was a shout from inside the house.

'Who is that? Who's at the door? Is it John? Johnny boy? Let him in!'

'Look what you've done now,' she said, her eyes bright

with tears that did not fall. Then suddenly she seemed resigned to his presence: 'He's got some kind of fever.' She stood aside to let him in, and as she did so he noticed that her normally slim body did not seem so tight any more, and he realized that far from letting herself go, she must be pregnant with her first child. Tom's illness had turned what should have been a happy time for them both into a nightmare. His own wife had been expecting a child before her untimely death, and he knew that women in that condition often had ups and downs in their moods, which came about through the adjustments being made in their bodies by nature.

Tom was sitting up in bed. His eyes were bright and there was a flush to his cheeks, which were an unhealthy looking red. He was starting to swing his feet over the side of the bed.

'Johnny!' he said as Carter entered. Carter gripped his deputy by the hand.

'Tom, what's all this? You're giving your good lady some grief?'

'The old man, he'll get killed without me!'

'Go get the doc,' said Carter quietly to Beth, who stood in the doorway, 'it's all right, I'll pay personally. Get him to bring some of his knockout juice.' Beth hurried off with a look of relief on her petite features. She had obviously been too worried to leave her husband alone.

In the meantime Carter did something that soothed his deputy as no other medicine might have done: he sat in a chair beside the bed and told Tom about the posse, and how they had patrolled the Tulloch spread to put the fear of the devil into whoever was trying to scare off the old man. He opened a window, too, and let in the cool air of early evening, and this, combined with the flow of conversation, seemed to ease Tom's mind. The doctor came and gave the young man a concoction of brown liquid containing laudanum that went down with ease, and Tom, looking tired but satisfied, slipped back underneath the bed sheets and drifted off to sleep. The flush on his cheeks was fading, and he no longer looked so feverish.

'I never thought I'd say this,' said Beth as she stood with Carter at the front door, 'but I'm glad you visited. He was fretting about the whole business, and you've eased his mind. On the other hand, you caused the problem in the first place, which I'll never forget. But thanks.'

He left with mixed feelings, and hoped that Tom would be a lot better when they met again.

To his amazement, just as he went towards his resting place – his quarters beside the office, where he had stayed, or rather existed, since the death of his wife – Rebecca stepped out of the very alleyway in which he had sheltered earlier, and stood in front of him. To his surprise she was not looking angry with him any more. Instead there was an enigmatic half-smile on her pretty face, and a look of weariness.

'I'll be getting a reputation around here,' she said, 'a hussy and all that, after the good sheriff. Can I speak to you?' It occurred to him that the street might not be a good place to have a discussion. It was early evening and the streets were quieter, but after what had happened earlier that day he was not going to wait too long out in the open. He hitched his horse to the rail without saying another word and went up the step to the raised boardwalk, unlocked the door to the building, opened up, looked back briefly and walked to the interior. She got the message and followed him inside.

This time she did not say anything when he offered her coffee but waited until they had a mug each of the beverage. He pulled up a spare chair and sat across from her.

'What happened when you got to Zeke's?' she asked.

'Nothing, except when we went in to see him, the strangest thing occurred, in a personal way.'

'What was that?'

'It was as if knowing we were around had put some fire back into his soul. He was sitting there polishing a rifle – a Winchester '73, but not just that – he had a flintlock from before the Civil War, two kinda rusty Colts and a Henry rifle. He was oiling 'em until they looked as if they were in good working order.'

'He's biting back,' she gave an involuntary laugh. 'Old Zeke's not going down without a fight.'

'I just think he wants to prove that he ain't finished yet. And you know what? I don't think he even cares if they get him in the end.'

'Who are "they"?'

'I don't know yet, but I'm working on a theory. It's my job, after all, and they made it personal when my deputy was attacked. Now I want to know why you're here.'

'I just couldn't stay away from the wonderful John Carter.'

'Now, we both know that ain't true. You can't wait to get this job done and get out of here.' He looked at her shrewdly. 'I guess you found out about ornery Southern businessmen today.' She winced and he saw that his words had hit their mark.

'It was not the least bit easy. I went to speak to storekeepers, the doctor, the town clerk, and a few others. Most of them were perfectly pleasant, but at the end of the day they told me nothing, and that town clerk. . . .'

'Jason Johnston, I know him well.'

'What an obnoxious little man! Made it plain he wasn't going to give me his time because I was a woman, and he didn't think he could waste a moment on me. I have never had the desire to punch anyone before, but in his case I would make an exception.'

'Yes, Johnston does reach a new level of annoyance.'

'And he leered at me as well, as did one or two of the others.' He did not point out that as an attractive woman in an area like this, far worse could have happened to her. 'So that brings me to you, Sheriff.'

'I don't know what I can tell you.'

'Sheriff, I guess you know that you are closer to this whole thing than anyone. I was going to wait, but there's no point. What do *you* know about the elections?'

'It depends what you want to know.'

'Just tell me, I think the time for games is over now.'

'No, I won't.'

'Then I'll have to contact the governor.'

'You misunderstand me. I've been riding all day, besides having to run for my life. I smell like a hog and need to get cleaned up. How's your hotel? They serve food at night?'

'Why, Sheriff, are you asking me for a date?'

'I guess so. Now get on your horse and I'll join you in a few hours' time. Then I'll tell you all you want to know, within reason.' She capitulated, knowing that she had won a minor victory that could help her advance her cause.

'All right, I'll be expecting you.' He led her out of the building. It was still early evening, and he made sure she was on the mare that she had hired for the duration of her visit. She turned and looked back: 'Be there,' she said.

'Get to your hotel,' he said, 'it's different for women around here. There's some real bad guys going around.' Then she was gone. The hotel was on the outskirts of town near the coach stop. He wasn't too worried about her, but he meant what he said.

He had not told her, but he was feeling weary, it had been a long day and the attempt on his life seemed a long way off. But he hadn't waited long in front of his office. Because of the time of year the days and nights were roughly of the same length and it would get dark fairly quickly. The town would be lit soon by those establishments that were still open – the saloons, the barbers, the food shops – hanging oil-filled lanterns outside their premises. He would do the same before he left to spend some time with the young woman.

After an hour of sleep that he badly needed, he had a good shave with a cut-throat razor, a good wash, and changed his clothes. The activity was quite soothing, and his mind was filled with thoughts of the young woman he was going to meet. He did not conceal from his mind the fact that he was seeing this as more than just a business meeting. She was attractive, she had big eyes and she would listen to him.

The bitter pill was the elections. What was he going to tell her? Some home truths crossed his mind about his own behaviour in getting Jim Knott to the position of power in this key town on the south-west trail. Many things were on his mind now, but he pushed them down, and decided he would tell her exactly what she needed to

71

know, but would not compromise anyone he knew.

Having finished his preparations he filled the oil lamp, made sure the wick was trimmed and lit, and then went back into the office, where he put on his black cotton coat and jammed his hat down on his head. Time to go. His horse Dagwood was safely bedded down for the night in its stable, because that way, he figured if he had a drink or two he could freshen up with a walk on the way home. He took one of his guns, of course, but stuck it into the depths of his coat pocket. Hotels tended to frown on people bringing guns into their public rooms in an open fashion, thinking it was a little disquieting for the other patrons.

Then a thought came to him. He had been attacked in his own town, and it had happened after the arrival of the young woman, when people already knew that she was looking into possible vote rigging. If this was proven, then the ramifications could be huge – like the removal of the mayor and a re-election. Certain parties had colluded to make sure the elections would happen, so could it not be the case that they would try and silence the one man who connected them all together?

A cold sweat broke out on Carter's forehead. He had been so bound up in the events of the day. Barney Sullivan might have a grudge against the sheriff, but that was personal. If Sullivan wanted a fight he would do it in the good old-fashioned way by marching up to Carter and swinging fists. Or, if he wanted the sheriff dead, Barney would challenge Carter to a duel in the sun, to see who was the fastest draw. Sniping at a man from the top of a hardware store was not his style. Carter knew he had been clutching at straws, refusing to see what was in front of his face.

At that moment a change came over him. He would tell

the truth – as far as he knew the facts involved – about the elections. Then she could decide where her investigations were going to go before the inevitable showdown with Jim Knott. What was more, he had always looked on the businesses and political masters of Destiny as his friends – but now he wasn't so sure. Well, this meeting would lay it bare, and he suppressed a thought at the back of his mind that involved expressing other feelings that he was developing for the woman he was about to meet.

He locked the office, looked at the oil lamp with a degree of satisfaction – it should still be burning on his return – then began to walk towards his fate.

CHAPTER NINE

The sixth sense he had developed over the years that he had been a lawman stood him in some kind of stead, otherwise he might have gone under right away with what happened next. The town had quietened down now that it was approaching dusk. As he walked towards his destination a man came walking out of the shade of the porch across the road in front of the very hardware store from which the shots had come at him that morning. The new arrival could have been anyone who was out for a stroll, as many people were after their work in various parts of the town, except he wore a bandanna that was red with white spots, and it concealed most of his face. The disguise was made complete by the hat pulled down low upon the crown of his head.

Rather than get into a fight with such an individual, Carter decided that he would keep walking until he was around the corner, where he could duck into the shadows and draw his gun. There was a sharp bend in the street and once he was around this, he was going to confront the stranger.

But just as he thought this, there was a soft scraping

against the dusty road and two men dressed in a similar fashion to the first, faces well concealed with bandannas, came out and stood in front of him.

Carter did the most natural thing in the world and reached for his gun, but the man who had been approaching from the hardware store knocked the weapon out of his hand before he could use it, and the Colt went spinning towards the boardwalk.

Carter ran forwards and straight into the arms of the two men who had appeared from around the corner. It was obvious that they did not intend to shoot him – that much was clear from the beginning. But this didn't mean they were going to treat him with kid gloves.

He was a strong, athletic individual, but even so, his day had been a long and weary one, and he had been looking forward to a little rest and relaxation with a pretty woman, all of which meant his reactions were not what they might have been earlier that day. The two men in front seized an arm each, while the third punched him on the back.

Even so, Carter was so big and strong that he nearly managed to break free. Unluckily for him the blow that landed on his lower back and connected with his kidneys causing an excruciating pain to shoot through his body and he sagged in their grasp. But his weight was so great that they let go of him anyway, and he fell to his knees in the rutted roadway.

As he knelt there they fell upon him. There was nothing about the rules of boxing here: he simply felt a flurry of blows hit his body – his shoulders, his sides, and the back of his head.

With a supreme effort, and uttering a howl that might have been made by an injured bear, Carter turned, and with a brawny arm, took the legs out from under one of the men. The man gave a grunt and sprawled on his back on the road, his head hitting the boardwalk with a distinct thud. This meant that Carter had space to manoeuvre, and he wasn't long in taking the opportunity this offered. He sprang forwards at a crouch and managed to stagger to his full height as he went forwards.

There was no time for him to hesitate: he turned, and showing that he was no mean hand at employing his fists, managed to get the hardware man a punch on the side of the head that sent him reeling.

The third and last man was soon taken care of because Carter smacked him squarely in the middle of his face, hearing a satisfying crunch as he broke the man's nose. It seemed that the mighty Carter was managing to come up on top again.

There would, of course, be the trouble of arresting the three men, but once he got his gun back – and he could see it lying a few yards away – they would be in gaol in no time.

As he went towards his gun ready to pick it up and bring this farce to an end, the man who had been lying on the ground sprang to his feet, the rest apparently having done him some good, and jumped on Carter's back. Carter did not fall to the ground, but he was certainly bowed over by the weight, and staggered about like an old man.

'You broke my nose,' said one of his attackers in a bubbling manner that suggested he was talking through his own blood. 'Bastard, you're going to pay.'

Broken nose and hardware man closed in on him and began to punch him in the ribs, and he caught a glancing blow on the cheek that hurt as much as the ones to the lower part of his body. He sensed that they weren't going to kill him, but they were out to teach him some kind of a lesson – but he had a feeling he wouldn't be going dancing for a while after they had finished.

Then he gave a desperate heave and managed to dislodge the smaller man, who slid off his back. The three of them had created a small circle around him and were taunting him the way that hunting dogs might taunt a bear, but he was still on his feet, and with a growl like a bear he rallied his strength. He had mighty arms, had John Carter, and a punch that had knocked out many men. Despite the hurts of his body, if he was able to make just three good connections he would lay them out.

Then there was a whine like a suicidal mosquito, and hardware man leapt as if he was performing the early stages of a barn dance as the dirt kicked up at his feet. Another of the men cursed as a bullet passed so close to his body that it tore the shoulder of his waistcoat and grazed the skin beneath. The three fell away. This gave the desperate sheriff the chance he had been looking for, and he dived for his gun.

By this time the three men had turned, and were running around the curve of the street – evidently getting shot at was not part of their contract. There was some kind of scrambling to get on their waiting steeds, and by the time Carter had managed to scramble to his feet, weapon in hand, he could hear the already distant pounding of horses' hoofs.

He stood there for a brief moment, then made some kind of decision in his head and headed back to his office, grateful for the attentions of the unknown sniper.

When he finally turned up at the hotel Rebecca was

waiting for him in the main atrium. The Grand, as the business was known, was mainly used by travelling businessmen coming off the stagecoach. It was not the most impressive hotel he had ever been in, though he hadn't been in many: the decor was dingy, with brown being the predominant colour.

'You're late, she said, but there seemed to be no real ire in her tone. It was starting to get dark and the look on his face was enough to draw her attention.

'What the heck is going on? You have a mark on your cheek.'

'I'm not going into details,' he said. 'I came here tonight because I owe you that much, and to give you a warning.'

'What about our meal?'

'Meal?' the word seemed to draw from him a faint outpouring of scorn. 'I'm afraid we'll have to put that one on hold, Miss Becky.'

She looked at him rather strangely.

'Why don't you explain what happened tonight, I'm an agent, I think I'll understand if you just talk. And I can help.'

'You can't help with this, leastways not in my books. I've got some advice for you, agent Seymour. Right early tomorrow you pack your bags, get on a coach and get out of here. Bring in your big guns if you have to, but just go.'

'But *why* in the name of God, what's this all about?'

'I don't know, I really don't, I only know that it's getting dark and I've got to go. Listen to me: I'll check up on you in at least a couple of days, if you're gone, fine.'

'I'll come with you, wherever you're going.'

'No, stay here, I mean it, and get that first train out of

town. It's not safe where I'm going, but it's safer than here.'

'Johnny.' For a moment her eyes held his, and then she stood up on tiptoe and kissed him on the lips. Even in the state he was in, a faint smile came across his broad face and he gripped her body for a short while. She pulled away from him, an unspoken promise between them that when this was all over they would exchange more than a hurried kiss.

His roan was hitched outside the building, laden down with a pannier on either side. He had prepared well for his departure. He heaved his big body into the saddle with a little bit of effort like a man carrying a burden up a steep hill and rode off into the gathering dusk, leaving behind the one person who at this moment in time seemed to be on his side.

He rode quickly and efficiently along the trail that led out of town. On the south side were a series of hills that ran up the side of Jim Knott's ranch. These hills had not been claimed by any of the settlers because they were useless for farming or cropping, but they had the merit of being fairly green and heavily wooded.

John Carter had known this area since he was a boy, and once a mile or so from town he led his horse to a valley between two of the bigger hills and walked the reluctant animal up a slope that took him to the place he wanted to go. He urged it onwards because now the light was almost gone and he did not want to be stranded out in the open.

He smoked, which was lucky, because now he lit a match and set fire to a handful of dry grass. The dark scent of the smoke was intermixed with the rich smell of the pine trees. The light was enough to show that he had arrived at the cabin in the woods, his secret retreat, the place he had always gone to when he needed time on his own.

The aches and pains that he had concealed so well from Rebecca now almost overwhelmed his body. He forced his reluctant frame to take just a few more steps, stumbled into the interior, and collapsed on the ground.

The young rider was supremely confident, as many young people are before life comes along and gives them a beating, He was tall, well dressed and in good health, with an arrogant mind that said he could do what he wanted.

He also knew a little secret.

Sheriff Carter had been seen riding out of town. There had also been a few witnesses who had seen the beating that the sheriff had taken the previous night but who were too scared to do anything. One or two had said something about gunshots from nowhere, but he had dismissed that talk as coming from their imaginations.

The departure of Sheriff Carter from the town was the sole reason why the rider was now mounted on his horse and riding the trail towards the JK ranch, except that he wasn't going to the ranch itself, but was heading for the hills. He was conscious of a certain excitement in the back of his mind, and it was the reason he was alone. Carter was a problem that had to be dealt with, and it was better if one person did it alone.

The best of it was, Carter probably thought that his hiding place was safe, that he had a retreat, and in a sense this was true because not many people knew about the cabin in the woods. Jim Knott did, though, and the young man was closer to Knott than most. Knott, of course, wanted the problem dealt with, and he, too, favoured the direct approach.

The hills were quite beautiful at this time of day. The ranks of pine trees that sprang from their steep sides in such profusion gave off a rich, almost heady scent. A low mist was swirling around, and there was a fresh breeze that blew the smell of grass and pine around the young man as he came to the spot where he wanted to be, and dismounted.

He tethered the horse to a low branch just in case it wandered off or was startled by a racoon and took off at a gallop. It was a long walk back to town, and he had not yet had any breakfast, bar a couple of coffees, so eager was he to get on with his self-imposed task. Once he was finished he would go to Herb's and order hot waffles and beans, all fried up and greasy. He could feel his mouth watering already.

The walk was a hard one, which took him up high on a path that had been blazed between the trees. He was amazed that Carter had managed to do this when it was nearly dark, but then he guessed that pain and fear could drive a man to do a lot more than he might manage normally. Then from below he caught sight of the cabin. It was quite disappointing – he had imagined something much grander, but this was little bigger than a shed. He paused, took his bandanna from around his neck and tied it around his face. He slipped his gun into his hand and resumed his climb.

This was nothing personal, he said inwardly, but beneath the makeshift mask a slow smile spread across his face. Carter would be dead, and most people would never know what had happened to him in this remote spot.

Then Knott could employ a new sheriff, one who would toe the line for the sake of his health – hell, he might take on the job himself.

He swiftly climbed up to the cabin to end this farce, and get back home for breakfast.

CHAPTER TEN

When Carter came back to some form of consciousness he thought maybe some twenty minutes had passed, but he wasn't too sure. He lit a candle and went out to where Dagwood was still waiting, looking a little sorry for himself. With what remained of his strength he took off the saddle-bags and threw them inside the cabin, then led the roan around the back of the building. There was a makeshift shelter there consisting of a frame with a roof, a kind of basic stable. He gave him some oats and molasses and threw a blanket over him to keep off some of the night chill, said a few reassuring words to him as he patted him on the neck, then staggered back into the cabin, pulled out his bedroll, wrapped it around his body and slept like the dead man they wanted him to be.

The next morning when he awoke he felt as if a demon had taken up residence in his body and was poking him with a red-hot fork, only this one had many more prongs than the traditional three. His face was sore and the back of his head felt as if it was making a determined effort to fall off.

His ribs were sore to the point that every time he took

a breath a sharp pain would shoot through his entire ribcage. It showed how exhausted he had been, that he had been able to get any sleep at all. Gingerly he felt his ribs and decided that they were bruised rather than broken, and as he got out of his bedroll and tried carefully walking, the pain eased a little.

His legs were painful too, and his lower back and shoulders were sore from when they had been pounded the previous night. He felt hellish, and probably looked it, too.

He had no facilities for making hot food. Usually when he was here he brought food with him, hunted for small game, and cooked what he caught on a spit over a campfire in front of the building. Instead he drank water from one of the canteens he had brought with him. He didn't feel hungry, but forced himself to eat some of the bread and cheese he might formerly have fed to his prisoners.

It was still early in the day, and this gave him time to reflect. Far from seeing his retreat from the town as a cowardly act, he looked on it as the chance to get away from forces who wanted to harm him. Just a few days ago he had been a man who was well thought of – but now he was nothing but a liability, and inside his own head he was able to consider the one word that made this so: knowledge.

He was the one person in the town who knew what was happening with the businesses there, between the cattle barons who so dominated the area, and the deals that they had made with the land reformers and the railway companies looking to purchase land for prospective routes. Not only did he have the knowledge of what was going on in the town, and the area in general, he had turned a blind eye to what was happening that was not strictly legal in business terms. A blind eye? More like two, if the truth had to be told.

The cabin contained one chair, a rickety old thing that creaked when he sat down on it, and a table. He reached into one of his saddle-bags and produced a bottle of scotch. He was not much of a drinker, but a drop or two of the liquid the Indians quite rightly called firewater ought to be enough to ease his aches and pains. Enough, and he might become completely numb. He put the bottle on the table, with the prospect of what he was going to do looming in the near future.

Unlike many of the townspeople he was supposed to serve, he was made of stern stuff. He turned his back on the bottle and the tin mug from which he was going to drink its contents and walked painfully out of the cabin to stretch his body and take some deep breaths of fresh air.

The winding trail that led up to the building did not do justice to how steep the incline was on the far side of the cabin. At that point there was only a ravine that led straight to the heavy growth of trees below. Coming out on the shallow side he was lucky that he was able to live to fight another day. A bullet sang past his head and buried itself deep in the wooden structure of the building. A more foolish person would have ducked back inside the cabin, but that would have meant he was trapped. Instead he quickly took stock and ran around the back of the building with the intention of gaining access to the woodland and disappearing from sight.

This chance was denied him when another shot rang

out and disappeared into the greenery, showing that the person was close behind him. He quickly moved to the other side of the building. On this side was the minor ravine that led down from the rocky base on which sat the cabin.

Instinctively his hand went to his side, but he had left the building, foolishly, without having his gun belt strapped on and in his gun belt were twin holsters that contained his guns.

Unbidden, a curse arose to his lips.

He was in no danger of falling into the ravine, deep though it was, due to a stony area several feet wide between him and the steep drop, but even so he flattened his body against the side of the cabin, feeling the roughness of the wood against his back. Now his bodily aches and pains were forgotten and instinct was telling him what to do. Then a man with the lower half of his face concealed by a 'kerchief came running around the corner, gun in his right hand, which was the closest hand to Carter.

Carter simply reached out and brought one of his mighty fists down on the man's shoulder. If the blow had landed properly he would have broken the bone, but because the man was turning at the same time, Carter's fist bounced off his body. Even so it must have been enough to send a numbing shock down the man's arm because he gave a loud gasp and dropped his gun. He was sensible enough not to scrabble for the weapon but pulled back from Carter's clutching hands.

There was a stand-off as the two men stood and faced each other, their bodies tensed for an opportunity, then Carter lurched forwards with another roar of rage and frustration, and clutched at the tall but slim cowboy; he grabbed him by the arms and began to swing him towards the edge of the rocky platform on which they stood.

The cowboy realized what was going to happen and with a desperate heave, managed to free one of his hands, which he balled into a fist, using this to give Carter a thump on the head. This was not well aimed since the latter was shaking him about like a rag doll, but it did catch him on the forehead, causing Carter to see a number of colourful and interesting constellations. The blow also snapped his head back and he let go of the other man's arm.

The stranger was young and lithe, and managed to run for his weapon, now lying in open ground to the side of the pair. Like a man doing a few health exercises at the start of his day, he squatted down and scooped up the silvery gun. He almost didn't manage to get upright because Carter was moving swiftly towards him, but with an extreme effort of will he did so, and retreated away from the sheriff.

'Sheriff, you're a dead man,' he said and began to raise the weapon – but as he did so Carter gave another earth-shaking roar and ran forwards, the sight of which made the young attacker retreat backwards so that he could aim his weapon. This was a mistake, because he immediately real-ized that he was teetering on the edge of a sharp fall. He gave an involuntary cry of fear, rage and panic all rolled into one, and flailed his arms as he tried to keep his balance – but it was to no avail, and his screams echoed around the brooding hills as he fell downwards. There was a crashing and smashing as his body hit the dense undergrowth – and then he was gone from sight, and there was nothing but silence except for the sound of early morning birdsong and the laboured breathing of the sheriff, on his knees at the edge of the precipice.

CHAPTER ELEVEN

Rebecca was still in the Grand Hotel. She had not packed her bags, and she was not going anywhere, which was what she had decided, so first thing next morning she went to the sheriff's office, thinking Carter might have changed his mind. This was an extraordinarily law-abiding town for a number of reasons – the vested interests made sure that they kept trouble down, the cattle barons who really ran the town kept a tight rein on their men, and most of all, the sheriff and his deputy were good at making sure that troublemakers were run out of town or jailed as quickly as they appeared.

However, she was startled to see a man amongst the busy early morning pedestrians who was heading straight towards her. It was Jim Knott, and from the look on his face it was obvious that he was not intending to have a pleasant chat about the latest fashions.

'Miss Seymour? I'm glad I've caught you.'

'Where's Sheriff Carter? I was going to meet him and continue with my work.'

'I'm afraid you won't be meeting with Sheriff Carter, he has departed for pastures new.'

89

'What do you mean?'

'Any sheriff who turns on his own citizens, and we've plenty of proof, is dangerous and out of order. He'll be tracked down and brought to justice. He is not a suitable person for you to deal with. There has been some amount of corruption in public office. When did you last see him?'

'Last night, he was talking about leaving, but I didn't think he would do it.'

'Yes, well he has taken off leaving his position vacant, although I believe young Tom will soon be well enough to take his place, and we have no problem with that particular public figure.'

'Where does this leave me? I've been asked to find out what happened at the fall elections, and no one is answering my questions.'

'You could have asked me.'

'I beg your pardon, Mr Knott, but at this particular moment I shouldn't even be talking to you about anything, given that you are the very person I'm investigating.'

'That might be the case, young lady, but I guess you'll need some help. I will get young Ralph to accompany you and you can ask any questions you want. I ain't got nothing to hide, and with his help you'll get all the answers.'

'That doesn't seem right to me.'

'I guess so,' Knott shrugged, 'the businesses in this town, they get so they clam up if they think they're bein' investigated. Wouldn't matter if they were being asked about their profits or the price of buying stock, they just think it's nobody else's business. I promise you, this'll be our last conversation.'

'Even if I was to accept this offer, what did you do to the sheriff?'

'Carter's finished,' said Knott, 'he's been attacking his own people, as I say, and when Ralph gets back he'll help you out.'

Rebecca was tempted to tell him that she was with the Pinkerton agency, and that she knew a lot more than she was pretending about his election behaviour – but if she did, she knew she might be throwing away her one trump card. She needed Knott to believe she was just an election official sent by the state.

'And when you finally come to see me, my official paperwork will be available for scrutiny. Nothing will be denied you. Well, it's been pleasant talking to you, Miss Seymour,' the mayor raised his hat politely, and then walked on. Looking at his retreating back, the young woman had a feeling that she was being ushered into a trap from which she would not be able to escape.

She went back to her hotel to await the arrival of Ralph – and she would have a few words to say to him whenever he turned up.

She kept waiting.

Once he had recovered from the lone attacker, Carter got to his feet and made his way into the cabin. His aches and pains were still there, and his bruised ribs made his breathing a great deal more laboured, now that all the adrenalin from the fight had vanished. He knew with a grim degree of certainty that he had disposed of a well connected young man, a young man who might have been acting on his own initiative, though Carter seriously doubted that this was the case.

He wasn't going to have time for that scotch after all. He packed some of the goods he had brought with him, and went to the makeshift stable at the back of the cabin. He fed his horse some more oats and fresh grass that he gathered from the trail, and gave him water, too.

Once more time was against him, because when they – and he now knew who 'they' were – discovered that Ralph was missing, he would be hunted down without mercy as if he were the worst outlaw who had ever lived.

Even doing a simple thing like putting the saddle on his horse's back was a strain, but he managed to do it, then tightened the cinch straps, making sure the saddle was firmly in place on top of the horse blanket. The roan might turn out to be his only means of survival, so keeping him comfortable and well was a sensible thing to do.

Although his body was aching from the attack, the fact that he had been moving about had eased some of the stiffness, and he found as he led his horse down the steep trail that led to the plain below that he was able to move with a great deal more ease than before. He had made a decision that might cost him some time. Leaving his horse tethered to a branch – he couldn't take any chances on it wandering off, or he was surely dead – he went into the woodland at the point where it descended from the side of the cabin. There was a degree of self-interest in what he was doing, because he wanted to check if the body was actually who he thought it was.

Regardless of his self-interest in gaining that knowledge, his brain was working overtime telling him what he had to do. This was Jim Knott's territory, and he knew that the mayor was a thorough man who would do whatever was needed to track down the man who had once thought of him as a friend. This meant that he couldn't stay around here, as Knott knew every inch of the land and would flush him out eventually – which meant that Carter had to reach an area beyond this territory.

He was just approaching the part of the woods where he thought the body might be amidst the dense under-growth when he paused, lifted his head and listened. Mixed with the usual animal sounds – the scurrying of small game, birdsong, the burbling sound of the stream that ran through the hills – he could hear a sound like thunder in the distance, a sound that he knew from expe-rience. It seemed he had even less time than he had thought. He cursed briefly under his breath, turned, and made his way quickly to where his horse was waiting, climbed a little painfully into the saddle and took up the reins.

'Dagwood,' he said, 'you've got to be real good to me,' and he began to ride, hardly needing to spur the horse onwards, such was the rapport between man and beast.

For the present he remained at the base of the hills, a clear idea in his head of where he was going, even though he knew he might be putting himself in danger to get out of danger.

He was heading towards Pleasant Valley.

The sound of those pursuing him was closer than ever. He looked back and saw them in the distance. Two men who wore bandannas over their faces and had their hats pulled down low just like the ones who had attacked Tom just a few days ago. The fact that they were concealing their faces was an encouragement to him, the very act of doing so meant that they were afraid of being exposed for wrongdoing, and were therefore acting in pursuit of someone who was still very much a representative of the law.

That didn't stop either of his pursuers from having a gun in one hand while they held the reins with the other. Neither did it stop them from loosing a few shots at him that if they had hit home would have got him in the back.

He did not draw his own gun – not for the moment – because he knew that it was notoriously difficult to twist around in the saddle and shoot anyone chasing behind without running the risk of the horse becoming skittish and throwing its rider. Instead he rode low in the saddle like a jockey, head down over his horse's mane, his whole body flattened out to follow the line of the animal's contours so that he made himself less of a target.

It was no comfort to him that most of the shots aimed at him went wide because there was always the danger that his horse could be hit, and that would be an unmitigated disaster.

After what felt like hours of pursuit, but was only about twenty minutes or so, he saw that the landscape was changing in a noticeable manner, dipping downwards as he entered Pleasant Valley.

This was a place of rills, gullies, dead ends and passes, where the hills ended and the Missouri river deepened as it took in a number of streams and waterfalls from the hills above. The terrain was green and grassy with a number of cottonwood trees growing together in clumps near the water. It was at this point that his worst fear was realized. The two gunmen had been concentrating on riding as they descended into the valley, but as the terrain eased off one of them took a shot that missed Carter but took his horse in one of its back legs.

Dagwood gave a whickering grunt of pain, stumbled to a halt and began to fall to one side. Divining what had happened, Carter immediately freed his feet from the stirrups and threw his body in the opposite direction. He knew what it would mean to be trapped beneath half a ton of horseflesh – he might suffer broken bones, and even if that didn't happen he would be trapped and helpless when the gunmen arrived.

The hapless animal grunted in pain as it fell heavily on its side, while Carter managed to push his feet against the barrel-like body of the horse and lever his solid frame on to the green path beside the river. He did not even hesitate, but ran as hard as he could towards the nearest clump of trees, only looking back once he was in some kind of shelter. His horse was still writhing on the ground, grunting and whickering and trying to get up.

Carter knew he might be sealing his own fate, but he couldn't see the animal suffer like that. He drew out his gun, calmed his mind by a supreme effort of will, and shot the horse in the head. Dagwood made one more convulsive sweep with all four hoofs, whinnied loudly, and died on the spot.

The two men pursuing him immediately reacted by riding hard towards the trees where the sheriff was hiding. He had no time to think but loosed off a few more shots at them, all of which went wide of the mark because his opponents were in constant motion. Then he ran out of bullets and had no time to draw his other weapon because they were nearly upon him. He did the most sensible thing in that case, turned and ran off in the opposite direction, soon becoming lost in the trees. However, this was not woodland as such, but merely a growth of cottonwoods – he could smell the rich loam that was stirred up by his boots, and his nostrils were filled by the green scents of the leaves and grasses around him.

The problem for the men chasing after him was that they had never been here before, but when he had been sent to challenge the Sullivans the sheriff had taken note of the lie of the land. He had not been here for over a year, but he seemed to remember that the uneven landscape descended into a gulch that filled with water when the river was high. The gulch, torn out of the landscape like a bite out a giant cake, was uneven and filled with stony outcrops that had been created by the ceaseless influx of water over the years.

He took a turn off what little path had existed through the woodlands, and veered off to his right, trusting in his memory and hoping that he was heading in the right direction.

Then he was there, right on the edge of a steep slope, while in front of his startled eyes there appeared a deep depression in the earth that reached to the side of the river. The slope was steep enough to give him pause for thought, but he could still hear the two men crashing through undergrowth behind him, and that meant they would be visible in seconds and he might lose the element of surprise. He teetered for a moment on the edge, then began running downwards.

It was one of those decisions that once made, seems like a huge mistake. One moment he was standing there, and the next he was running down a slope at such a breakneck pace that if he tried to slow down he would probably have fallen and broken his legs or arms or both. It seemed certain that he was about to hit rock bottom, and then he would break something anyway when he tried to come to a halt.

Luck was on his side in one respect, and not in another. At the bottom of his fifty foot descent there was a kind of plain that was covered in mud where the water had seeped through from the river. His running fall ended when he landed in the muddy bottom and fell face forward. He struggled to his feet gasping for breath, and was glad that he could not see himself in a mirror, strongly suspecting that he would look like a chocolate statue.

The mud was glutinous and clung to his feet, but luckily he was wearing long riding boots and the suction was not powerful enough to pull them from his legs. But he had to keep going, though he felt as if his whole body had been slowed down to a tenth of its normal speed.

In front of him were some of the stony outcrops he had seen earlier, and the walls of the gulch were rugged with plenty of indentations. The men who were chasing him would be able to draw on him from above, but once he was in the shelter of one of those minor caverns he would be well protected and able to fight them back.

He pushed forwards, his speed increasing as the mud dried up and gave way to a firmer surface, and then he was able to run between the stones and hide within shelter. He had heard one shot since he had arrived down here, and that had hit one of the outcrops.

This told him that he had reached shelter just in time. The determination of those following meant that they were not about to just give up and leave him alone.

He was feeling weak, thirsty, and incredibly tired. He had used a great deal of his strength just getting down the slope, and now that he was resting all his bodily aches had returned tenfold. Weakly he reloaded his empty gun, took out the other one and made sure that this, too, had enough bullets. He crouched against the shallow wall of the cave like a waiting bobcat. They weren't going to take him.

'Reckon we'll have to go down there,' he heard one of the men say, the voice strangely familiar.

'Hell it's a steep 'un, we could end up hurt real bad.'

'He seemed to get down all right.'

'Then I guess we'll have to try.' On hearing these words he braced himself for the confrontation. There was going to be a shoot-out for sure.

Then suddenly there came the firing of shots from a rifle, which made a distinctly different sound from their guns. Carter dared to creep to the edge of the cave and look upwards. He was distant enough from where they were to be able to look back up the slope.

His pursuers were standing with their backs to him now, hands up, facing some new arrivals.

'What you boys doing on my land?' asked a harsh voice that had lost all trace of an Irish lilt. With an inward groan he recognized the voice of Barney Sullivan. 'Now you got one minute to persuade me not to acquaint yore brains with the outside world courtesy of a bullet from this here old Henry.'

'Barney, it ain't what you think,' said the taller of his two pursuers, whose voice he definitely recognized. 'Fact is, we're here chasing after a renegade sheriff. Someone who you got no cause to love, nor none of us, fer that matter.'

'So, cut out the mystery, boys, afore I get my men here to take upon themselves to give you a shake or two to make the facts drop out of you.'

'Sheriff John Carter,' said the second, shorter man. 'He's turned traitor to his own town and everyone that made him. He's right close by – if you just let us flush him out like the sewer rat he is, we'll dispose of him right good and be on our way. We'll even take the body with us just to make sure he don't pollute your land.'

'That ain't gonna be the way of it,' said Barney, reasonably enough thought Carter, who was listening, as might have been expected, with close attention. 'We'll take care of this, me an' the sheriff, well we have a history you might say, and me and my men, well we know the lie of the land better than any of you Knotty boys.'

'You don't know who we are,' said the taller man.

'Soon find out when the lead tears you apart,' said Barney, still in that reasonable tone of voice, which had the effect of making the two intruders back down.

'OK Barney, you win. We'll just go back to where we belong, if that's all right with you,' said the taller of the two. His companion tugged at his arm.

'Burrows, the boss said we was to get him.'

'Idjit, shut up. Barney here, he's got the men and the need, he'll do us a job.'

'Sure will,' said Barney, 'he's dead meat. Now get on your horses afore I change me mind, boyos,' the last few words said in a mockery of his long since abandoned Irish accent.

Neither of the men who faced him was under any illusions of how precarious their current situation was. The pair of them hastened to leave, and the next thing Carter heard was the sound of them going back through the clump of trees from which they had emerged.

'Now let's see what we can see,' said Sullivan. Carter

ducked his head back inside his makeshift shelter with a sickening certainty inside that he was not going to be able to stay there for long.

'He can't stay down there forever,' said Sullivan, 'you men cover the other side and I'll wait here. Looks as if we've got us a little task today.'

CHAPTER TWELVE

The two men who had left the task of disposing of the sheriff to the Sullivans were riding comfortably back to Knott's spread.

'Idjit,' said Burrows, who had discarded his makeshift mask now that there was no one to see them. 'You nearly got us shot there, Lambert.'

'I was just trying to do my job,' said Lambert, who had also discarded his own disguise, 'but I guess with a guy as unpredictable as Sullivan you don't take any chances. So I guess it's time to go back.'

'Not yet,' said Burrows. 'See, I had an inkling young Ralph was going to steal a march on us. Thing is, Carter was making tracks when we saw him. Reckon what we do is ride past the hills and see if we can find any signs of Ralph.'

'Aww, that'll take us well out of our way, not what was ordered at all.'

'Lambert, if you had the brains you were born with an' did the planning, we'd all be in bother.' Lambert rode onwards with a sullen air and did not talk to his companion. His damaged nose might have had something to do with this. In a way, Burrows couldn't blame him – they had been riding hard all that morning, and had been shot at by a man who had a need to protect his land that bordered on being deranged. In fact it was only by leaving Carter to Sullivan's tender mercies that they were alive at all.

As they came closer to the path that led to the cabin in the hills they came across an animal that immediately raised concern, and quickly banished the sullen air that Lambert had been wearing for the remainder of their ride. Ralph's horse was coming towards them without a rider, and from its broken reins it looked as if the animal had been tethered but had finally managed to break free. It was a spirited youngster and had not liked being tied up in an unfamiliar place.

Lambert captured the gelding and tethered him to a branch along with his own animal. Burrows too dismounted and they immediately began to search in the woodland. It was fortunate for at least one person that they had returned, for they soon heard groaning noises and a parched cry for help coming from the bottom of the minor ravine.

They broke through the thick undergrowth and found Ralph lying in the middle of a large bush, part of the tangle of greenery that had helped to cushion his fall. It was fortunate he was a young, slim man, because if he had been any heavier the fall might have broken his neck. As it was he had obviously broken one of his legs and perhaps damaged a couple of ribs.

'Well,' said Burrows, who had ridden the trail many times and had often bound damaged limbs, 'guess we'll get you strapped up and git you home.'

'Where's Carter?' asked Ralph hoarsely, a feverish look on his face.

'Carter's dead,' said Lambert, 'or as good as.'

Carter wasn't dead, but he knew that this might happen at any time. He was still armed, which was a testament to his own foresight, but he was in a desperate situation. He had not been able to see how many people Sullivan had with him. He could wait where he was and defend his position, but to his own mind this was not really something he wanted to do. It would not be long before he ran out of bullets, firing from where he was, and then he would be trapped and the end would be inevitable. He decided instead, now that he was on firmer ground, to try and get out of the branching gulf in which he had found himself.

He had been able to rest for a period of time, and this meant that his strength was a little renewed. He had also gained some time because Barney had said he was going across to the other side of the huge gash in the earth. With this in mind Carter knew that he had only one choice. He crawled out of the cave – his canvas trousers were already badly besmirched – so that he was less of a target for whoever might draw a bead on him, and made sure that he kept close to the uneven walls of the gulch. A little further on, when no shouts came, he got to his feet and began to run. But at once he heard hoarse shouts from more than one person, and knew that he had been spotted. More than one pistol was fired and he heard shots whining off the rocks and could smell gunpowder. No doubt if he looked back he would have seen smoke on the rises above, but this was not something he was about to do.

He concentrated on the uneven ground and ran as fast

as he was able, gun in one hand, the other one holstered so that he had a free hand to grasp any projections in case he stumbled and fell. All it would take was one mistake and he would be dead.

Fortunately it seemed that Barney had not been able to make his way to the other side of the gulch as quickly as he wanted, and there was no one there to prevent Carter getting out. He was also helped by the fact that the slope on the other side was far gentler than the one down which he had descended so rapidly just minutes before. Once out of the gulch the greenery was as thick as before. His mind was working overtime as he ran up the sides. If he could get into another thicket of trees, if he could keep up the pace, and if he was able to hide successfully or fight off his pursuers, he might be able to survive long enough to get out of Sullivan territory.

A lot of 'ifs' and very few certainties.

He emerged from the gulch. If he had still had his horse he would be free by now, but it was pointless dwelling on what might have happened if that had been the case. Just the same, there was a rising anger in him sparked by what had been done to the best horse he had ever owned, an animal that had helped him through long days of riding in the sun, which had always been steady and had helped his master at every turn. He had not just lost an animal, he had lost a friend.

But he did not have time to dwell on this either, because the greenery in front of him – tall fir trees and thick bushes – suddenly came alive, and out of the place where he had been looking to shelter came a group of young men and women, about ten in all (not that he was counting), ranging between the ages of six and fifteen years. Some of them had sticks, some bows and arrows, and one of the older boys had a Winchester rifle slung across his shoulders. Carter had heard there was a tribe of Sullivans, and that their children were feral, and now he was faced with living proof of this supposition.

The group, who looked as if they were hunting game, were as surprised to see the sheriff as he was to find them. He was still on the edge of the gulch and he now had two choices: he could go back down to where he had come from, or he could run in the opposite direction, because although he was armed he was not so far gone that he was going to fire on children.

Carter did not have much time to make up his mind because the group gave what can only be described as a collective whoop of joy, and began running towards him. He did the only thing that he could, and ran in the opposite direction. They were younger than him, and fast, but there had been a good distance of many yards between him and them when he had been spotted, and he had started running as hard as he could. His legs were still strong, and he was tall, and he widened the distance between his tired frame and those chasing him quite easily.

The only trouble was that, fast as he ran along the trail beside the gulch, he soon encountered a big, black-clad brooding bear of a man who had dismounted from his big gelding as soon as he had seen him. That figure was Barney Sullivan. Behind him two of his men remained mounted on their steeds, but pointing rifles straight at him. From their strong resemblance to their leader it was clear that they were two of his many sons. Carter had heard somewhere that the Sullivans had eighteen children, all of whom had survived to adulthood, so their presence was not too much of a shock.

'So it's yerself,' unexpectedly Barney gave a wide grin. It made him look like a bogeyman who liked to eat small children. 'Sure I would put the gun down, Sheriff, it makes me boys trigger fingers itch, and they like target practice.' Carter lowered his gun just as the whooping, cheering grandchildren of the Pleasant Valley despot arrived.

For the young woman waiting in the hotel there was nothing but a nagging doubt that she was being treated like an idiot, and the feeling galled her. She knew very well that when young Ralph turned up he would be perfectly charming, would take her around the businesses and to the mayor, and she would get the answers she wanted, that there was nothing wrong with the election process, and they would send her on her way. Then for the town, it would be business as usual. There wasn't a thing she could do about it. She would just have to do what she was told.

In fact it was time-keeping that saved her. She detested people being late, always filled her time well, and Ralph did not turn up within the promised hour. She decided that it was time to go out on her own after all, the one question on her mind being what had happened to Sheriff Carter. This time, for her safety, she had decided to fetch her mare from the stable at the back of the building. There was a hitching post at the side of the hotel, and she was around the corner from this, heading for the stable, when she heard the sound of hoofs and horses being halted.

'This one stinks,' grumbled a low voice, which she was able to pick up with her sharp hearing.

'I guess so, but it's what we promised to do.'

'Well, now the Sullivans have got Carter he'll be dead by now, so it's time to dispose of her. We don't know what he said to her before he left.'

'Stop that talk! We're here to take her around just like Ralph was supposed to.'

'Yeah, we're real gents,' said the first speaker, who sounded as if he was not relishing the task. Being around the corner from them was probably the most dangerous thing that had ever happened to her. If they really wanted rid of her they might just shoot her on the spot, if they knew she was intending to escape. She flattened her body against the back of the building. Her heart was hammering, but she wasted no time. As the men departed to go into the hotel she went in through the back, went to her room, which fortunately was on the ground floor, grabbed clothes and money, and headed back out again before the desk clerk came to look for her.

She got to the stables and managed to get changed quickly into more suitable clothes in the very stall where her mare was kept. It wasn't a thing a young lady should do, but she was not going to be treated like an idiot any more. Once changed, she left her old clothes in a heap, saddled up the mare and led her out, jumped on board, and rode away from town as hard as she could.

'Get it over with,' said Carter, waiting for the inevitable, 'just shoot me through the heart, make it quick.'

'Granpa, kin I do it?' asked the boy of barely fifteen, an eager expression on his youthful features as he raised the Winchester and pointed it at Carter.

'Put it down, sonny,' growled Sullivan. 'I have a few questions before we skin this one alive.' His two sons

107

behind him grinned at this supposed joke, revealing that dental hygiene was not at the top of their list of priorities as they showed blackened and missing teeth.

'You've had your laugh,' said Carter, 'but I've never harmed a single one of you.'

'You threatened us,' said Sullivan, 'you came here and tried to lay down the law. Now it looks as if the law is the outlaw, sure, so we ain't got any reason to keep you alive.'

'I guess.' Carter looked curiously at Sullivan. 'You haven't killed me yet, and I know you well enough to realize that you don't really preserve your enemies just for the sake of it.'

'Yay, you've heard the story sure of how that Hogan and Knott made a foray into here in the early days, tried to take some of me territory. Well, the four cowboys that was found hanging from a tree all pretty like in a line, for sure it was a good warning not to mess around with the Sullivan clan.'

'So why am I still here?'

'Sure, the ould sherrif is wondering why he hasn't become target practice,' said Sullivan, roaring with laughter and sweeping a hand towards the man who stood there, a giant amongst these strange twisted people, but overwhelmed by their numbers. The two sons and the children shrieked with a kind of mad glee, and Carter realized that he was a diversion in their strange lives.

'Put it like this,' said Barney, 'if Jim Knott has taken the umbrage against his wee golden boy there has to be a reason. Tell me the reason and I might be inclined to be a wee bit lenient.' Carter looked around – he was trapped and helpless. He could lie and bluff, but the truth was just beneath the surface, and it was the truth that came out.

'Last fall, elections were held in Destiny. A few candidates came forward, but the main tickets were for Marty Hogan and Jim Knott,' his throat seemed to grow tighter and there was a sound of hammering in his ears that seemed to grow louder and louder, the sound of his own heart thundering inside his head. His breathing was shallow and he felt a wave of dizziness sweep over him. 'I helped them, I helped his men vote, and I blocked access to some of the ballot boxes. I turned people away from places where they could vote. I was the reason Jim Knott won the election.' When he had finished he stood there totally demoralized, feeling worse than he had ever felt in his life. Death was nothing now, he knew what he was, and that was worse than any punishment.

'Well, well,' said Barney, 'a confession. Not the kind of thing ye'd expect from a man of the law, looks as if Jim boy has a good reason to see you disappear, him and Marty too, if truth be told. Put yer guns away, man, it's time.'

'I might not go quietly,' Carter drew out his other gun, 'I've nothing to lose. I'll take you with me!' It would be his last, sudden act of defiance.

'Don't be stupid, big man. I'm not going to kill you. I'm invitin' you to dinner.'

CHAPTER THIRTEEN

The Sullivan spread was at the top of Pleasant Valley. It was built more like a fort than a traditional ranch, with high fencing surrounding the building. The ranch itself had a central building and a wing on each side, reflecting the fact that the huge Sullivan clan had to have somewhere to live. Barney said nothing as he and his sons – who were called Lorcan and Mikey, Carter learned during the journey – had him walk between their mounts until the building came into sight.

In his heart he could not believe that this was happening, but as he entered the gates he found himself standing in front of the biggest ranch he had ever seen in his life, and decided once more to accept his fate.

He found himself in an enormous drawing room which did not contain enough furniture for the number of adults and children who floated around the place. In a daze he was introduced to a plump, dark-haired woman who still showed traces in her face of the stunning beauty she had once been.

'Molly, me wife,' said Barney. 'She's the real boss.'

After this, preparations were made for a meal, and this was prepared by the women of the family, including the wives of Barney's two oldest sons.

Carter had always pictured the lives of the Sullivans as being primitive, as basic as they come, with the people of the family living in not much more than mining camp conditions, with brutish men and sluttish women. In fact this way of life was richer and a lot more wholesome than that of most of the families who lived in Destiny.

The meal was simple, consisting of a choice of chicken, steak and fish, accompanied by vegetables and potatoes, and followed by pints of beer. The men ate together and the children were fed elsewhere. Carter had been given a change of clothes – a striped shirt and jeans, that fitted him reasonably well since many of the Sullivan men were as big as he was.

He ate some of the food put in front of him, but his head was low and he avoided eye contact with those around him.

Arguments flew back and forth between the men at the table, but mostly concerning the upcoming cattle drive to Texas and the fact that they had to give Hogan and Knott access through their land – an agreement that had been made many years before between the respective parties, but the price of which Sullivan had milked to his own advantage.

Barney finally asked Carter to speak with him alone in a room that had been laid aside especially for the patriarch. They sat on chairs that had been made more comfortable with cured cow hides. Barney sat down with a grunt and offered a cigarette to Carter, who accepted it gratefully since he had not smoked since leaving town.

'Well,' said Barney, 'we've been known to punish those who come into our land without a by your leave. Ye'll be wondering why I preserved you. But it is as simple as I said: my enemy's enemy is my friend. Now it looks to me as if you're a thorn in the side of certain people. What are you going to do about it?'

'I don't know,' said Carter dully. He was still feeling devastated by his confession. Barney looked at him shrewdly and chuckled loudly.

'So ye took some money to sort out an election. You won't be the first and you won't be the last.' At last Carter was roused to some sort of anger.

'You're wrong, old man, I never took a cent for what I did. That wasn't why. It was for Jim, I thought he was my friend, I thought they all were.'

'All of 'em?'

'The businesses who asked me to help get him elected. I didn't actually create false ballots, but the way I worked it they knew that he would get elected.' Carter passed a hand over his eyes. 'I really thought Jim was the best person for the job.'

'Best of it is, son, he probably is. Doesn't matter who gets elected, they always swing it their way. So how would you like to go on?'

'What do you mean?'

'Well, I guess I'm asking ye for somethin'. You see, those sons of bitches, they think between 'em they can push people around, helped by their land-grabbin' and their deals with the railway companies, who're going to start building round here real soon. Ye could help me and my kin and get rid of these tinpot despots, or ye could run.'

112

'Run?' Carter had eaten well; he had smoked, so he felt more like his old self. His head snapped up and he looked the elderly man in the face.

'Sure, ye could get a horse and ride off into Texas. A fine man like you, change your name and set up as sheriff in some other town. Wouldn't be hard to do.'

'I suppose so.' The prospect was tempting, just to run away from a prospect so dire that he had to fight from giving way to despair. 'But I've already decided I ain't giving up. I wouldn't give them the satisfaction. Not now that you've given me a lifeline.'

'We're goin' to drop you off at the one place they won't look for you.'

'Where's that?'

'Oh, ye'll see, me boyo.'

Zeke Tulloch sat up wearily at the sound of horses' hoofs. He had been wearing himself to death just acting in self-defence, or at least getting ready to do so. He ate whatever food he had stored, including dried beef, and drank wine, water and beer, also stored for his own use. He slept in his clothes and didn't change very often. He was surrounded by his weapons, and at the moment he was more at risk of causing harm to his own person than the enemy, from the number of times he handled his guns.

He crawled to the window, rifle in hand, and was startled to see a group of the Sullivans – some four in all – riding up with a fifth man in the middle whom he recognized immediately. He didn't know what kind of trick was being played on him, but he had no arguments with the Sullivans, who very much kept to their own.

That didn't mean to say that they hadn't formed some

sort of alliance with his enemies. However, the presence of the sheriff was a little comforting. The only problem was, Carter was not exactly protective of land rights, and he had shown more than once that he was on the side of the big cattle men. Tulloch, of course, had not heard the latest news.

Barney Sullivan waved a white flag and came forward with Carter at his side.

'It's all right, man, just thought I'd see ye for a little while.'

'What do you want?' yelled Tulloch barely lifting his head above the level of the window sill.

'We thought ye might like to give the sheriff here a wee bit o' shelter for a few days,' said the Irishman.

'Why?'

'He'll explain himself, trust me boyo, it's quite a story.'

'All right, I suppose. The rest of you, just leave.'

'Sure, that was the plan all along. All right boys, let's light out of here and leave these two reprobates alone.'

'Thanks,' said Carter, in a low voice. Barney gave a booming laugh.

'Carter, I ain't doin' this because I like ye. You were an enforcing bastard for Knott, and as far as I'm concerned you're only here because you can do me some good, while killin' ye would help that brickhead Knott.'

'It doesn't feel that way.' The patriarch shook his head, got back on his horse and gave a hand signal to his hulking, grinning sons. They all left, the pounding of their horses' hoofs against the dry soil raising a real dust cloud as Carter walked forwards. They had left him the horse he had ridden to Zeke Tulloch's place.

Tulloch waited a good long time until he was sure the

other old man was out of sight, then unbolted his door and appeared with a Henry in his hand. It was the kind of weapon he would have used during the Civil War, and one that he felt comfortable with.

'What the hell were you doin' consorting with them Sullivans?' he asked, 'and what do you want with me?'

'I need to lie low for a couple of days,' said Carter grimly, 'else there's a risk of getting my head blown off – nearly happened a couple of times, too.' The look on his face was so stark that Tulloch immediately bolted the door again.

'Who's after you?' he asked fearfully.

'Half the town by the looks of it, but they've no reason to suppose I'm here. All I ask is some shelter for a couple of days, and believe me, man, you'll get the full weight of the law behind you to save the ranch once I've dealt with this situation.'

Tulloch hardly had enough time to take in or appreciate what was being said before they heard the sound of another horse's hoofs on the hard, dry ground.

'Place is turning into a regular way station,' grumbled the old man. Both men seemed to be in total agreement without the need to exchange a single word, because Carter went to the left side of the building and Zeke to the other, each crouching down at one of the sealed windows, Zeke clutching his beloved Henry and Carter pulling out one of his pistols. From the sound he knew it was only one horse, but he was still taking no chances.

Carter was the first to look out. He lifted his head for a second, caught a glimpse of a grey-clad figure, wearing a hat with a bandanna covering the lower half of its face.

He ducked down again, fully expecting there to be a

shot smashing through the glass at any second, but nothing happened.

There was a knock at the door.

A knock at the door was not normally surprising, even in the life of a lawman in this part of the world. But it showed the trauma of the last couple of days that even this innocent act seemed like the trump of doom.

Swiftly he crossed to the entrance, undid the primitive bolt and quickly, in one smooth and flowing motion, threw the door wide revealing the grey-clad figure standing expectantly in the open doorframe. The figure stepped forwards, and Carter grabbed it by the loose cloth at the front with his free hand and pulled it forward swiftly and remorselessly, noting at the same time that the person was much smaller and lighter than he had expected. The person in grey sprawled on the ground, pulled away the bandanna and glared at him.

'Carter,' asked Rebecca, 'is that how you treat all your visitors?'

He pulled away and looked at her with both shock and surprise written large upon his handsome but damaged features.

'Rebecca, I thought you were going away on the early morning train?'

'I stayed,' she said briefly.

'But why are you here?'

'It was the best place for me to stay while I was looking for you, especially now that you're not the only one running for your life.' The girl was on her feet now; she turned, and to Carter's astonishment walked towards Tulloch, grabbed him and gave him a generous hug that many a man would have envied. 'Hello Uncle Zeke, sorry,

I was too tied up to see you until now.' Zeke gave her a pat on the shoulder.

'Nice to see you, Becky,' was all he said.

CHAPTER FOURTEEN

Later on, getting towards the evening, the pair of them were outdoors, walking around the Lazy Z and checking what was happening to the ranch. Zeke had come with them at first, but had then elected to go back home and oil his weapons, once he was sure it was safe for the young woman to be with Carter.

'Uncle Zeke is my mother's older brother by quite a few years,' said Rebecca. 'My grandmother – what a strong woman she was – had nine children, and there was a gap of eighteen years between the oldest, Zeke, and the youngest, who was Mother. He set up here in Kansas a long time before I was born, when the Indians were still around, although they never affected his business, and he made a good life here. His boys are both dead now, and so is Aunt May, all of natural causes.'

They had been looking around and saw that the area surrounding the ranch was in a state of disrepair. Now they were walking back towards the rustic building.

'I think it's time for Zeke to leave,' said Carter, 'he's on his own, and he can't do much more here. His herds, from what I see, have dwindled to practically nothing. He sure as heck won't be doing another cattle drive.'

'No, you need other people for any enterprise,' said the girl, 'even when it comes to the law.'

'What do you mean?'

'That night, when those men attacked you, I was there.'

'What do you mean?'

'You were taking so long to come and see me I decided to see if the tough Sheriff Carter had chickened out of a date, and answering a few questions. Three men were attacking you. I decided to help you turn the tables, so I slipped out my handy little Smith & Wesson .32 and had a crack at them.'

'I didn't see you!'

'I was in the shadows further along the street, but they were lit by the circle of oil lamps around the businesses in that area.'

'You were the lone sniper.'

'I sure was. They train us to shoot at the agency, you know; I'm a pretty good shot. When I saw you had everything under control I slipped away, figuring you would see me in your own good time. I didn't think you would take off like that.'

'That was a practical decision based on the fact that another sniper – who I presume wasn't you – had tried to kill me from a rooftop the previous day. After the second attack I guessed that if I hung around Destiny I was going to be history as much as the Indians. You saved my life.'

'You saved mine, because you put me on the alert. So when Jim Knott offered me the services of his son who never turned up, but two of his thugs did, I figured that I, too, was going to be part of history, hence the reason I'm here. Why, what's wrong?' She saw that his face was working.

'If they had harmed a hair on your head I would have gone in there guns blazing, I wouldn't have cared what happened to me.'

'Why would you do that?' He halted and turned towards the girl; he put out his left hand and cupped her chin, put his other arm around her and drew her towards him, leaned forward and kissed her on the lips. She paused for a moment then responded softly and sweetly. He put both arms around her, and she pressed her firm body against his. He could feel her large breasts against him and she could feel his arousal. She drew away from him, but her expression was far from displeased.

'John Carter, I didn't think you felt that way. Not here though, we'll have plenty of time when it's all over. Besides, those cattle are watching us.'

'The hell with them,' he drew her closer, kissed and held her again for much longer. When they finally parted they were both a little breathless. They returned to the ranch and Zeke looked at them sharply, and for the first time a smile played upon his old tired features, though he said nothing.

Rebecca was very efficient. She found the food supplies that the old man had in the ranch, lit a fire in the grate, and altogether made the place a lot more homely in a short time, getting Carter to chop wood and help her clear up. She also cooked a fine meal for the three of them, with some salted pork, beans and corn, and she even managed to make a loaf of bread using ingredients from Zeke's storeroom. She also managed to scold the old man into having a wash in the old tin bath in water heated over the leaping flames of the fire, and got him a clean change of clothes.

Zeke seemed to have an endless supply of tobacco, and he took Carter outside while Rebecca cleared up. It was she who had chased them out of the building, telling them they would only 'get in her way'.

'Guess what we'll do is shelter here and make this a base for now,' said Carter, 'if you don't mind, Zeke – then we'll see about fighting back. Killing a sheriff is a mighty serious business. With the help of some sound men I use as my deputies, people like James Bell and Ron Curran, I can bring this situation under control.' He had been so absorbed in what he was saying that he had not been paying much attention to the horizon, but Zeke was always alert for trouble, and his eyes widened.

'I see smoke over there beyond that thicket of trees. Someone's camping over there and they've lit a fire.' Carter saw the wisps of smoke now, in the far distance, a long way from the ranch.

'Cowboys out herding likely,' said Carter, but he was now on high alert.

He did not have to say anything more, as the sound of hoofs could be heard in the distance.

Where the ranch was situated there was a fence of sorts, although it was rickety and broken in places, and a main gate also made of wood. It was at least something that could act as a barrier. Without any discussion the old man and his younger companion ran forwards and fixed the main gate in place with a large piece of wood on stays, which acted like a bolt. Zeke would have been hard pressed to lift this by himself. Once it was in place it would have taken a battering ram to shift the main gate, though that still left the problem of the broken fencing.

They both rushed back into the building, barring the main door there and pushing the windows open at the front. Hearing the noise, the girl came running through from the back where the kitchen was, and stood there in the flickering flames of the fire and the candlelight – for it was properly dark in the interior now – and looked at the two men.

'We might be facing a final siege,' said Carter grimly. 'Get back, crouch down or go somewhere safe.'

Rebecca did not hesitate. She still had her gun with her, and it was not without the bounds of possibility that whoever was approaching might try to get in at the back of the building. She rushed through to where she had been cleaning and drying the plates, cups and cutlery used for their meal. Zeke had not been in the habit of doing this; he had simply eaten off the same plate for weeks, giving it a wipe with an old cloth when it became too greasy. She took her gun out of her bag and stood beside the back window, breathing deeply.

'Zeke!' yelled a voice at the front of the building. The ranch owner dared to lift his head above the line of the window and gaze out. Four men in dark clothing sat there atop horses that shifted uneasily, sensing what their owners were about to do. 'Zeke,' said the rider furthest to the left, 'you go see Marty Hogan and Jim Knott. You sell your land equally between the two of them. You'll get a fair price.'

'Who are you?' demanded Zeke. It was a fair question, since all four of them were hiding their faces behind ban-dannas.

'That don't matter much,' said the speaker. He had to yell because they were all ranged in a row beside the main gate and the lower fence that was still the height of a man.

'I ain't having truck with anybody,' yelled Zeke. Carter did not say anything – he wanted there to be an element of surprise if it came to a fight.

'Is that your last word, Zeke?'

'Why would I have any truck with a bunch of murderin' thievin' polecats, cowards too?' demanded the old man.

'Well, don't say we didn't warn you,' said the masked leader with deceptive mildness. He turned his horse and the others followed suit, and they galloped off to where their camp was situated.

'Well, that was easy,' said Carter, 'too easy.'

'Why don't they just kill me and have done with it?' grumbled the old man.

'Because they know that if you're found dead or go missing the US marshals will have to be called in,' said Carter. 'The first thing they would do would be to look at who has to gain out of this, and that would be the two ranchers just mentioned. They don't want that. But worse, you don't have anyone you can appeal to locally. Not now that I'm dead.'

'You ain't a ghost, far as I can see.' For the first time in days Carter allowed a slow smile to spread across his broad, usually good-natured features.

'You're right Zeke, and that's what I'm counting on.'

'Are they gone?' asked the girl coming through, 'that was a lot easier than I expected.'

The calm was not to last. Even as they stood there they could hear the sounds of whooping and yelling that had been used before to frighten the old man, and once more they took up positions ready to fire at the invaders.

This time though, in the evening twilight, the four men were carrying burning torches and they whirled them through the air at the building – two at the front and two at the back. Then, still shouting and hollering, they rode off.

The old ranch was a much different prospect from the feed shed they had attacked before. The main building was constructed mainly out of wood timbers, and dry as timber could be, while the several outhouses and the barn were of lighter construction.

'The grass. . . !' said Zeke, with a gasp of horror. He did not elaborate on the word, but threw the front door wide and they were able to see what he meant. It had been a hot summer just after the rains, and the grass around the ranch, which would usually have been cut down by his stockmen, who had now all departed, had grown lush and long in the rain, and had then wilted and dried in the sun. Because it had never been allowed to grow to this extent before it had never been considered a danger, but each individual blade of grass acted like a stick of tinder, and the torches, their blazing heads coated in pitch, had set them alight and the fire was spreading rapidly. The smell of the burning rose through the air, along with clouds of low-hanging smoke.

The biggest danger in Carter's eyes was the ranch building. It was over forty years old and the timber had been painted a dark brown at some point with creosote to preserve the timbers. The creosote had done its work well, but unfortunately it was also a fire hazard because it would cause the wood to burn easily.

Carter did not hesitate. This was a problem to which he

could respond and act upon.

'Water, did you get any during the rainy season?'

'Sure did,' said Zeke, 'them butts at the side of the building were all filled' – this was common practice in a business where water was an essential part of the daily working life.

It was as if Carter and Rebecca had become one person, because she ran back into the building with him and snatched up the nearest cloth they could find – in this case Zeke's blankets – and ran back out. They all three soaked their bandannas in the water butt at the side of the building, put these on their faces and pulled their hats down low on their heads. Carter put in the first blanket and let it soak, the grey and black smoke billowing around him, then snatched the blanket out and started to beat out the flames as they approached the building. Rebecca and Zeke soaked blankets of their own and soon joined him in the fight against the encroaching fires.

It was a serious situation because it would take just one rivulet of flame to get a toehold on the old building and the whole thing would go up like a giant torch.

Luckily the wooden baton that had set the grass alight in this area had been facing the building. This meant the three of them were able to beat the flames down after Carter had picked up the torch and doused it in the water.

That was not the end of the matter because there was danger from all sides. So hot were the fires that were springing up at the outhouses and close to the barn that Carter soon found his blanket was dry. He ran up and soaked it again, and ran with the others towards the barn. This was the second greatest risk because it had straw and animal feed inside, all of which was completely dry. If the barn went up then the ranch would be at risk too, as well as the stables, within which the horses were jostling and making whickering noises as they caught the scent of burning fire and sensed the danger outside.

For an old man Zeke was heroic. He beat out the flames with the best of them, and they were into the third water butt before they were able to say, finally, that their work was done.

Once the flames were out, they were in near darkness because night had fallen as they were going about their self-imposed task.

They stood there panting with near exhaustion; Zeke looked around and crumpled to the ground, all his energy completely used up in this task. The young couple – for they were a couple now – helped him inside and made him comfortable. His blankets were ruined, but he had other coverings made of cow hide, and they waited for quite a while with him as he drifted off to a fevered sleep.

'This is entirely my fault,' said Carter when they were seated beside the fire. Ironically they had been fighting flames, now they were heating coffee over them, and talking in low voices.

'You didn't make them come here and attack an old man.'

'Remember that date we had, Rebecca? It all seems a hundred years ago now. Well, I was going to sit with you and give you nothing about the elections. But I have nothing to lose now, and I can say that those elections *were* rigged. We never actually stuffed the ballot boxes with multiple votes from one person or anything like that, but we made darn sure that the right people got in and deterred the rest. Seth Tatters was a big part of it, too. He arranged for some of the ballot boxes to be in his bar, and he bribed customers with drink to go the way we wanted. It's surprising how many people you can sway. The result was that the local businesses got the mayor they wanted, and so did I. That desk in my office? It was a thank-you – all the local businesses clubbed together and bought it for their popular sheriff.' His voice was barely more than a whisper now. The girl had fallen silent for so long that he had to look up and into her face.

'I despise what you did,' she said, 'those elections were supposed to be free and fair. What about the other candidates?'

'That's the thing,' he could still barely face her, but forced himself to look her in the eye. 'Marty Hogan didn't really want all this election nonsense as he called it, but he did it for Jim Knott, to give him a credible opposition.'

'I don't understand.'

'No, and it's hard to explain. These men are powerful. They control huge tracts of land and employ hundreds, if not thousands of people in this area. They decided long ago not to horn in on each other's interests because it would cause too much trouble and cut into their profits.'

'So the whole thing was a sham? Jim Knott was always going to win?'

'Yes.'

'Would you testify to that effect?'

'It's my word against theirs, and a lot of people want to see me destroyed for even helping you – that's what this is all about.'

'That means "yes".' He tried to put his arms around her, but she drew away from him.

'Things are different; I don't know how I feel about

you now. You've caused me a lot of trouble, and they were going to kill me, you know. Luckily I'm trained not to have false hopes and think they wouldn't harm me just because I'm a woman.'

'I'm real sorry you feel that way.' Carter did not pursue the matter, but instead went on to another subject. 'Becky, if that was supposed to be a frightener for Zeke, that means they'll be back.'

'I was thinking that, too. If, as you say, they want some kind of answer, they'll return and see the damage they've caused and try to find out what he's going to do.'

'They nearly killed the old guy.'

'I suspect that was a miscalculation on their part, they just wanted to scorch some grass and maybe set fire to an outhouse. They didn't realize the brush was so high there was a danger of setting fire to the main building.'

'Well, I have an idea, but I'll need your help.'

She searched his face: 'Is it dangerous?'

'Probably.' He searched her features for any signs of hesitation.

'If it gets this over, count me in.'

'It'll wait until morning, early morning.'

They went to sleep in separate parts of the ranch. She took the spare room, but he bedded down in the front room in the bedroll Sullivan had supplied along with the horse. They drifted off with the smell of burnt grass and cloth in their nostrils.

She awoke in the early hours after a nightmare in which someone was chasing her endlessly beneath a blood-red sky, and got up and went through to where they had left Carter lying. She could hear Zeke snoring in his own room.

'Johnny, you can come through and hold me if you want,' she said, 'but no hanky-panky.' But there was no response, and in the flickering light of the candle she was holding she went over to the bedroll and leaned over. It was empty, and when she put her hand on the bedding it was still warm. That meant that just a short while before, it looked as if John Carter had upped and left her and the old man.

CHAPTER FIFTEEN

Carter had slept like one dead for about four hours. It was a secret that he never shared with anyone, but he could sleep for short periods of time and wake up feeling fully refreshed. What he did during the day was to take any opportunity he could to have a short nap of up to twenty minutes at a time, and this seemed to give him all the rest he needed. This meant that despite his aches and pains he could get up, dress quickly by the light of a candle, and make his way out of the building. The first faint traces of dawn light were showing on the horizon as he went to the stable and fetched the big quarter horse that Sullivan had supplied.

Still using the light of the candle he expertly put on the horse blanket, then saddled up. He got on the horse and steered it through a gap in the fence that he had noted earlier on, taking his time in the faint light. He let the animal go quietly across the grassland until he was far enough away from the Lazy Z not to alert its remaining occupants. Then he used his spurs and hurried the horse onwards.

On his way back to town he passed the place where the

encampment had been, near a clump of cottonwoods used for shelter. The blackened remains of the fire told their own story. The men must have returned to their own bunkhouses for the night, deciding to spend their evening indoors at their respective quarters.

When he arrived at the outskirts of town he tethered his horse to a hitching post near the hotel and made his way down into the town through the back streets. The increasing daylight, along with his expert knowledge of the streets, helped him find his way. Soon enough he was at the back of his own building. It was like stumbling across a piece of ancient architecture, so strange had been the events of the last few days.

But at least for now, the office was not his main aim. He crept along until he found Tom's house. There was a narrow window at the side of the building. He had with him his knife. The house had traditional shutter windows and these were not hard to open by sliding the knife through between the shutter and catch and pushing in the metal. Once this was released Carter lifted the shutter, but he did not follow this up by trying to climb inside. He had two reasons for not attempting to climb in, the first being that he was a big man and might well find he was stuck, the second that invading a house at this time of day was a sure fire recipe for getting your head blown off.

'Tom,' he said, rapping on the glass lightly but firmly, 'Tom. It's Johnny, I need to see you. Tom, answer me.'

From where he was standing he could see the doorway that led into Tom's bedroom. There was the sound of someone moving around, then the door opened a crack and he could see candlelight, although the interior was still shadowy.

Beth, Tom's wife appeared, a candle in a pewter dish in one hand, a pistol in the other aimed straight at his face – and he could swear he saw her finger tightening on the trigger.

'Hey, let me take that,' a figure appeared beside her and jogged the gun out of her hand and into his in one smooth motion. It was Tom, and he unceremoniously grabbed his young wife with his free hand and bundled her into the room. Given that she was pregnant he was only trying to protect her from possible intruders, but she gave a cry of annoyance.

'Who's there? Better answer fast, mister,' and looking at it from Tom's perspective it was easy to see why Carter was being asked the question, given that he could only see a pale oval of a face at the window.

'I ain't going to waste your time,' said Carter. 'Let me in, Tom.'

'Carter? What the hell? We thought you were dead or had gone off to Texas for some reason after you went maverick,' Tom said nothing else, but allowed the sheriff to slip in through the back door. Beth appeared at his side, now dressed in some hastily donned clothing while Tom stood there in his long johns.

'You look a hell of a lot better,' said Carter by way of introduction.

'Sure am,' said Tom, 'thanks to having the best nurse in the county. My side still hurts but it's a dull ache now that the scarring has taken.'

'Well,' said Carter, 'I guess I'd like to know what's been said about me.'

'Hell of a thing,' said Tom. 'People say you kicked over the traces and you tried to blacken Jim Knott's name.

132

Some unspecified folks took against you and tried to make sure you were on the receiving end of a bullet or two – and then you vanished.'

'Turn him in,' said Beth, 'he's no good, Tom. He's the one who got you shot.'

'Beth, I didn't actually fire a weapon,' said Carter mildly. 'Besides, I was here in town when Tom was attacked.'

'I don't know who you're in league with,' she said, 'but you're trouble, I want you out of here, if Tom doesn't arrest you and put you in gaol, that is.'

'Will you both give me a chance to speak?' asked Carter, trying to keep his temper down.

'We will,' said Tom, 'it's just a bit upsetting for my wife, in her condition, that you appeared like that. Come on, we'll fire up the stove, have hot coffee and talk.' Beth made them the coffee and had one too. Carter was aware that the daylight was coming in steadily and that he could not wait too long to make his request, but he was also aware that if he was too abrupt he might put his deputy – or maybe his ex-deputy – against him.

Now that they were relaxing a little he told them some of his story. He could see in the wan light that Beth was determined to remain against him, but when he mentioned that there had been a fruitless attempt to abduct and kill Rebecca she changed her look to one of grim anger.

'They were going to take the election lady and kill her? You swear on it?'

'Yes,' said Carter patiently. 'That's why we need to deal with this now, Beth. They say self-praise is no praise at all, but I was a good sheriff in this town, kept the peace and helped out everyone I could. I shot a few people, bad 'uns, in my time here and I helped send a few of 'em off to the county court for hanging, but I never hurt anyone who didn't deserve it.'

'The truth is,' said Tom, 'I was visited by Jim Knott just yesterday – in fact only a few hours ago, given the time of morning. He more or less said I was the new sheriff, would be acting in that capacity until there was a proper election, and that Curran would be my deputy, would give up his job in the hardware store and take up the post. Jim thought we could work well together.'

'Sure he did,' said Carter. He looked from face to face. This was a young couple with a bright future, Tom would do well in the post because he was hard working and diligent and he took direction well. The supposedly dead sheriff decided to regale them with a few home truths.

'Tom, if they can do this to me, they can do the same to you. Sure, you'll get the post and you'll do well, but there will come a point when you displease your political masters and then – well, you saw what happened to me. They think I'm dead. Well, I'm here because I believe in what the law stands for. I made a mighty big mistake not that long ago, helped bring in a man who used me, same as he's going to use you. One of these days, as sheriff, you're going to trip up an' they'll be on you like a pack of wild dogs. Believe me, I know.'

'Then I guess you'll have to ask me what you want done,' said Tom, 'and I'll see if I can help you out.' Carter had been expecting Tom's young wife to speak out against him, but her face was set as he made his request.

'They tried to burn old man Tulloch out of his property,' said Carter, 'and they're going to go back there today. You, me, the election agent Becky, we can bring this to an end. Tie up the whole business and show them up for what they are. Beth, it's not without risk,' he said turning towards the young woman, 'but I can tell you now, if Tom accepts this post of acting sheriff it will be a poisoned chalice.'

'Then I guess I'll do what I need to do,' said Tom, 'but my wife, she means more to me than anything. I don't want to risk what we have.'

'No,' said Beth suddenly, 'I never liked you, Carter, really, you're big and smug and seem to think you're the reason for the sun coming up in the morning,' and turning to Tom, she said: 'He talked down to you, Tom, he really did.'

'I did,' said Carter, a little shame-faced. 'I thought I knew it all, turned out I knew nothing.'

'So when are you leaving?' she asked her husband. It was his turn to look at her in astonishment. She hastened to explain her thinking. 'Put it like this, Tom. If you inherit this it'll be with you for the rest of time. If you help clear it up, you'll have a reputation, a good one.' That was enough for the young man.

'I'll do it,' he said.

Time was wearing on, and even though it was still early in the morning Carter had to be circumspect in what he was doing. A lot of people – riders for the ranches, travellers, hardware store owners, even the local doctor, and the countless labourers who made a town busy – would be getting up at sunrise and coming to work, and amongst them many people who worked for either Hogan or Knott. He did not want his face to be spotted before he carried out his plans.

Tom got dressed, had a hasty breakfast and went to the livery where he kept his horse. It was a big five-year-old and seemingly tireless. While he was doing this, Carter went to the outskirts by the same means he had used to enter the town, fetched his own horse and went on the trail, without his companion, towards Tulloch's spread, and waited in a clump of cottonwood trees. It was eerie waiting there with a fresh morning breeze wafting over him and the scent of the green woodland around him. In his heart there was also a fear that Tom, who had just agreed to accompany the obvious madman who had turned up at his home so early in the morning, would in fact turn up with a posse of the very men Carter was trying to oppose.

If that was the case they would have a fight on their hands. Carter had not seen his own face in a mirror for a good few days, but his mouth was more turned down at the corners, his eyes had lost the humorous sparkle that had always seemed to be in them, and he had lines etched at the corners of those same facial features which had not been there before.

He needn't have worried. Tom arrived shortly afterwards, and they rode to the Lazy Z in companionable silence.

They were met at the gates by a young woman who was bearing a Winchester rifle, and an old man who carried a Henry as if he meant business, both with expressions that showed they were not to be taken lightly, and who only relaxed when they saw who the new arrivals were.

'I thought you had abandoned us,' said the girl.

'I didn't have any time to give you an explanation,' said Carter, 'besides, you and Zeke were asleep. This was just something that had to be done.' He made it plain from his slow, deliberate speech and the way he caught their attention that he was in charge now.

'What's been happening out here is a key to everything that's gone wrong,' he said. 'If we can get together and do this, we'll be saving the future of Destiny.' His words seemed a little dramatic, but there was no doubt from the look on his face that he meant what he was saying.

Tom was looking at the scorched ground and the half-burned stalks of brush, along with the waterbutts that lay on their sides, empty when once they had been full. His eyes widened as he took it all in.

'So they've been pushing at you,' was all he had to say.

They did not have long to wait before there were signs that their attackers had returned. The smoke of a camp fire curled lazily up into the sky in the distance. They were not even trying to be cautious, believing they had only the old man to deal with.

'They'll be here real soon to talk terms,' said Carter, having already discussed tactics with the other three before this point had been reached. He truly believed that preparation was at least half of everything.

They had all saddled up by then, and the girl had donned her riding clothes, complete with hat pushed down low on her head. Carter looked at her with the lines on his face growing even grimmer.

'You shouldn't be coming with us, not with what they've been doing. The three of us will do.'

'What, an old man, a wounded boy and an ex-sheriff with aching ribs? I'm the only one who's fit for action!' This was so obviously true that he made no more objections. They had one advantage that the raiders did not, which was that Zeke had lived on his land longer than most of them had been alive, and he knew every method they could use to sneak up on the raiders. He took them to a place that seemed to go away from the area they were aiming for, a fold of land leading down to the river which ran through his property. The water was low, but the banks of the river were soft and not too muddy under the horses' hoofs, which meant that the sound of their movements was considerably deadened. They had already discussed the tactics they were going to use when they got there, but their main advantage was going to be surprise.

'Simple as this,' said Carter just before their journey, 'they were going to come back and confront Zeke, and ask him what he was going to do, and they expected him to give up and agree to sell his land. They won't be expecting four of us.'

The journey, though, was silent. The four of them came to another fold in the land that led up to the clump of cottonwoods where the criminals had established their camp the previous day. The party dismounted, all except for Zeke, who seemed to have some idea in his head that he was keeping guard over them, a grim look on his face as he clutched at his Henry rifle.

They moved up the hill and through the trees at the same pace, but instead of keeping together they were a few feet from each other. They all had their guns in their hands, Tom clutching a Remington, Carter with his twin Colts and Rebecca with her Smith & Wesson. The criminals were sitting in front of a camp fire, having evidently just consumed a cup of coffee each as empty tin mugs sat beside them. They were seated on the grassy uprising that led into the trees, this making a fairly comfortable seat.

Carter gave a hand signal to his companions and levelled his twin guns at two men he knew only too well, Jonas Burrows and Dick Lambert. Lambert had a damaged nose, which made him fairly sure he had been one of the masked attackers. It was no surprise that the other two men were employees of Hogan's, and that he had met one of them the day he was talking to that ranch owner.

'You're all under arrest,' he said. The men began to scramble to their feet, but there was a dry click as weapons were primed behind them and they realized Carter was not alone. However, Burrows was not one to give up easily. He dived for his gun belt, rolled away from them and headed straight into the forest, gun now in hand. Carter fired and there was a scattering of woodchips as his shot hit a tree near Burrows' head.

This was a bit of an upset, because the criminal would be able to fire at them from shelter, and it was the one situation Carter had been hoping to avoid.

Then there was a sound like thunder as the old man galloped his horse amongst the trees. He met the oncoming Burrows, and before the fleeing man could lift his weapon to aim at him, Zeke used his Henry like a club and brought it crashing down on the man's head, laying him out cold.

'That's fer messing around with my property,' he said.

CHAPTER SIXTEEN

Their operation had been a success. They got the other men to walk into town, with their wrists tied and all three of them roped together, while Burrows was flung over his horse's back like a sack of potatoes and carried in that way. None of them spoke that much as they walked along, but Elias, the tall rangy foreman, glared at Carter.

'I guess I shoulda shot better when I was on that roof.'

'You hear that Tom?' said Carter. 'We got us a little confession right there. Guess the law doesn't take kindly to folks who try to stop a sheriff doing his duty, and trying to murder him too.' Elias became silent, realizing the gravity of his situation.

'You ain't going to hold us long,' said Lambert, attempting a sneer, but not really succeeding, given the present company. 'Once Jim Knott gets to know of this you're all dead men – and woman.'

By this time they had reached the outskirts of town. What they were able to do next was possible purely because no one had been expecting the arrival of a man whom everyone thought was dead. Carter simply went to his old office, unlocked the door and unceremoniously put the four prisoners into a cell each, keeping them apart. Along with Tom he picked up Burrows, flung him on to the ground of a cell and dumped a pail of water on him. The prisoner sat up spluttering and saying some words that should have shocked Becky, but didn't.

'I'll see you later,' she said as they arrived. 'I have a couple of things to do.'

'Are you sure?' asked Carter with concern in his voice. 'This isn't over, not by a long way.'

'Don't worry,' she said, 'I'll be back very shortly.'

'All right, but watch out for danger, Becky.' With Tom as his witness, he read out to each man in turn their unlawful acts, having to do this several times because they began shouting and protesting and rattling the bars of their cells as he did so. The charges ranged from extortion – trying to make a man give up his land – to attempted murder of a sheriff, pursuit of said sheriff, and in the case of Burrows, wounding with intent to kill. Elias was also charged with the attempted assassination of a lawman on active duty. The other men were charged with aiding and abetting him to do so. These were not trivial charges, and juries in the South tended to look on anyone who tried to kill serving officers with a huge amount of disfavour. The prisoners would be lucky if they got jail sentences: probably all four of them would hang.

Since the prisoners had already eaten, he left them to stew, and with the help of Tom he took their horses away to the nearest livery, then went with his deputy for some food which they brought back to the building. He did not try to conceal his presence in the town at all.

On his return to the gaol he found Becky waiting for him; she had obviously returned to her hotel and changed, and looked as fresh and feminine as when they had first met. Nevertheless they all remained armed and alert, knowing what was going to happen very shortly.

Soon there was the sound of someone thumping on the door of the sheriff's office, which of course was locked as normal. The sheriff did what every sensible person does when they feel a sense of threat: exercising caution, he pulled aside a little wooden grid set in the door, and looked out briefly. Jim Knott was standing there. The presence of the mayor was all well and good, but behind him stood twenty or so men, ranged out along the road, most of them carrying weapons of one kind or another.

'Well Johnny, I never thought we'd meet in such circumstances,' said Knott. 'But I guess events make fools of us all. Let go of my men, and Marty's too, Johnny.'

'Guess I can't do that,' said Carter, keeping his voice calm, although the blood was beginning to hammer in his ears again. 'Looks like we got us a stalemate, Jimmy.'

'No problem I can see,' said Knott. 'You let my boys go, I'll let you live.'

'Your boys have broken the law,' said Carter, 'and so have Marty's, and they'll hang high enough to break their stupid necks. You've broken the law too, so I guess we'll have to draw you in at some point. Now disperse your men and go, else I'll have to see to you.'

'Ain't just my lot, half of 'em are Marty's,' said Knott. 'Our supposed rivalry was just a conceit we made up so that we could play the businesses against each other for more money, but we're of the same cloth. He's ill now, heart problems, but he knows you've got his boy. Now I'll ask you again, are you going to hand 'em over?' Carter's answer was to close the grille. He turned to his companions.

'Guess this means we're at war, time to get to work.' He knew that they did not have long, so he began to pull weapons off the gun rack, throwing them to Tom who loaded them with the speed of the young. They had a couple of Winchesters, their own weapons and some spare Colts. The young woman looked on with some bewilderment.

'I don't know what you're doing, the only way in is through the door or the two front windows. You have no way of firing on those men, unless you break the windows, and that wouldn't be in your favour.'

'You're all dead,' sang out Burrows from his cell, 'dead men – and woman,' and gave a high-pitched hysterical laugh that rang on and on, and rattled the bars of his cell.

'Shut up, scum,' said Carter, and rattled Burrows' fingers with the stock of his rife; Burrows fell back cursing and sobbing and nursing his bruised digits.

'We got us a little out,' said Carter, 'give us a hand with this, Tom.' On either side of the door were strong metal hooks. It soon became clear what these were for when he pulled a wooden bar from the corner and lifted it into place with his deputy, it weighed so much that the two of them struggled to get it into place.

'This ain't the way out,' explained Carter, 'just had to be done.' He pointed to the back of the building, between the cells. 'This bit's solid, made out of brick and concrete, but we sorted out an escape route, didn't we Tom?'

'This ain't the first time a sheriff's office has been under siege,' said Tom. 'They're kind of hot-headed around these here parts. When Carter was coming into office he devised a route that could help us get away real quick.' He did not spend any further time explaining the situation, but ran into the annexe of the building with Carter and they came back with a ladder, of all things, which they placed against the red brick of the wall at the back of the building. This prompted the girl to look up, and she saw there was a hatch on the roof of the one-storey building, bolted from the inside.

'They'll still get us from behind the prison,' she said.

'You get me wrong,' answered Carter, 'the time for running's long gone.'

He had to raise his voice slightly because all four of the prisoners were screaming and yelling imprecations at him now, while on the outside of the building the mixture of Hogan and Knott men were shouting for them to release the prisoners. Fortunately the noise was so great that it drowned out what the prisoners were yelling, because Tom literally ran up the ladder, slid the bolt open, and slid the hatch open.

'Zeke, you stay here and guard the door,' said Carter, 'you wait here too, Becky. If anyone tries to come through the window, shoot them. Zeke, I appoint you as my deputy and you are now serving me in an emergency capacity.'

'Sure thing,' said the old man, his eyes glittering as he turned to the yelling prisoners. 'All of you, shut your gaggies or I'll blow a hole in ye,' and he followed this up by loosing a shot from a pistol into Burrows' cell that missed that individual's head by a mere few inches and scattered fragments of brick from the wall that impacted painfully on the prisoner. They saw that he meant business and immediately became quiet. Burrows gave up completely and whimpered in a corner, knowing that Zeke had every reason to blow his head off his shoulders.

Hearing the shot from within, the first rounds were

released on the building; the sound of bullets ricocheting against the walls would have terrified most people and was not particularly pleasant even for the professionals. Zeke, though, had been through the Civil War and he did not look too troubled by the noise. He had lost his terror now that he had fighting companions.

In the meantime Carter followed Tom up the ladder. The thing they had not pointed out to Rebecca was that the roof had a distinct slope from front to back. That meant it was lower in the cell area, so when they emerged from the hatch they were invisible to those at the front of the building.

They spread out because the shingled roof was bowing a little under their weight, which meant it would be an ironic end for them if they crashed through and ended up with multiple injuries. The sun was beginning to rise above them now and it was going to be a fine day. They had both put on their hats to protect them from the elements, which was good because the sun was hot on the back of their necks. Both felt the sweat spring to their foreheads and there was a salty taste as they licked away the liquid beads that formed on their upper lips.

Becky climbed the ladder too and passed them up more weapons, so there was no danger of them running out of bullets, for the moment anyway. As they crawled upwards none of the men in the main street were yet aware of their presence, so they both dared to look over the edge of the slope.

At least half of the men had vanished somewhere, and Knott was standing back from the porch of the building on the road.

'You better release my men,' he said in a clear voice that

rang through the air, 'or you'll have brought the consequences on your own heads.' What those consequences
were became clear almost as soon as he said the words.
Carter had been relieved to see that some of the men had
dispersed, now he realised that they had merely gone to
fetch an object that immediately struck fear into his heart.
They were carrying a large log of stripped pinewood that
must have been obtained in the lumber yard on the outskirts of town. He did not have to be told what they were
about to do. In fact he and his temporary deputies Curran,
Bell and Grizzly had used the same method when attempting to get into a building where there had been an illegal
still. A lot of people made their own beer and even gin,
but a still that manufactured something resembling
whiskey out of corn mash could make its owners thousands of dollars and rob legal businesses of their revenue.
Anything that affected tax revenue was a kind of red rag to
a bull with the authorities, and was clamped down on with
great force.

It was no surprise to see that the ten men immediately
limbered up with their burden and charged at the door.
Carter had insisted the doors of the building were sturdy
and reinforced, but even the stoutest oak could only with-
stand so many blows.

As the battering ram came forward there was an
almighty thud that shook the entire building so that the
force of the blow travelled upwards. Tom looked over at
Carter, still looking to the older man for a guide to his
actions, and the sheriff gave a nod to confirm what they
should do next. They both steadied their guns and took
aim at the scene below. The trouble with doing this was of
course that it would immediately reveal where they were,

but they had little choice in the matter. While they were taking aim the battering ram hit the door once again with a tremendous crash.

The lawmen had an unspoken agreement between them: any shots that they fired would not kill anyone on purpose. Their reasoning was simple enough: the men below were being employed by Knott and Hogan, they did not know the full facts of the case, and probably thought their comrades had been illegally abducted, and they all believed Carter was a rogue lawman who had turned bad to the detriment of the town, or so they would have been told.

With a skill at shooting that came from long practice, Tom aimed at the soil between those holding the far end of the battering ram. He fired at the same time as his companion and the bullets kicked up the soil at the feet of those below while the guns made a terrifying bang as they were discharged. Most cowboys were used to dealing with cattle, roping and handling, and many of them did not carry guns as a matter of course, and were not used to being shot at – and this was true of the men who were trying to break into the building. Their immediate reaction was one of terror. They dropped the log and retreated from the scene.

All eyes were focused on the rooftop.

'The hell you say?' Jim Knott was looking up. Unlike his men he was armed, with a Colt .45 in either hand, and he immediately retaliated by firing up to where the shots had come from. The shots passed into the air because the two lawmen had immediately taken shelter by lying flat on the sloping roof. They had expected some kind of retaliation, of course.

'Pick up that thing and get to work,' ordered Knott, unable to keep the snarling rage out of his voice. They could hear, but not see him at this point, but the crashing of wood against wood and the shaking they could feel trembling through to their very fingertips was enough to tell them that the cowboys had resumed their work.

Carter nodded to Tom and held out a restraining hand, and then he quickly raised his head and fired again at those below, then just as quickly ducked down again a brief second before there was a flurry of shots at the precise point where his head had been. He could feel the heat of the bullets as they sang their way above his head.

In the meantime Tom carried out the same kind of attack, but from a different angle and this time there was a scream of pain as one of the men below was hit. He had not been aiming at anybody, but as far as he was concerned if anyone was trying to kill him they were now fair game.

The ram was picked up and the crashing of wood on wood resumed.

Tom started to raise his head, but was met with a flurry of shots that made him duck down again. Now that Knott and his men knew where they were they would hit them with holding fire until the door of the building had been smashed open. Carter tried to raise his own head and was met in the same manner. They heard shots from inside the building too, just after the sound of breaking glass. But the windows were divided by wooden supports and were not too large. Anyone who tried to break in through them would have to try and wriggle through – and Zeke was there to meet them with a few shots of his own, which is what it sounded like to the two men on the roof.

Carter heard a noise behind him and turned to see that Rebecca was on the roof after crawling out of the hatch.

'Get back down there,' he said.

'No point, they'll be through any second.' This was so obviously true that he didn't argue with her. 'I'm not staying here,' she added, sliding delicately down the roof, her skirts riding up and revealing that she had a lovely pair of legs. She really was a most attractive woman. Carter chided himself from having these kinds of thoughts, at the same time as wanting to protect her from her own actions.

'What the hell are you doing?'

'You'll see!' She had slid so far down that she had nearly reached the back of the building where the slope of the roof ended and the cell blocks stuck out at an angle. These were flat; she came to a halt atop one of these, threw herself over the side, dangled by her hands for a short while and dropped about six feet on to the ground.

'I'll be back,' she said, her face a pale oval down below, and she made off past the Chinese laundry and along the back streets, and was soon lost to sight.

CHAPTER SEVENTEEN

Carter suddenly realized that he had been an idiot. He slid down to the hatch.

'Zeke, get up here.'

'Ain't goin' nowhere,' said the oldster. 'Goin' to take out as many as I can.'

'Get up here now!' yelled Carter. 'We'll fight them even better up here.' Zeke looked up, his beard wagging on his old chin, but he saw the sense in what was being said and the crashing and splintering sounds from within clearly showed that the door was going to give way. Tucking his gun into his belt he climbed the ladder and joined his compatriots.

'Give 'em hell,' said Carter. He and Tom fired over the edge of the roof, aiming fairly randomly but keeping their shots within the area of the building. Then, as shots continued to fire above their heads they followed the lead shown by Rebecca just minutes before, slid down to the cell block roof, dangled from the edge and fell to the ground, after a second or two Zeke followed.

Carter was a big man and the descent to the ground jarred every bone in his body, his ribs felt as if they had been given a going-over by a professional boxer and his back, neck and shoulders were aching from the strain of being on the roof and raising his body from an unnatural position. His legs gave way and he began to fall. At that precise moment there was the sound of splintering wood and shouts of triumph as the battering ram did what it was meant to do and the door crashed inwards.

Tom stood by Carter with a look of concern on his face, but the older man glared at him.

'Get the hell outta here,' he said. Tom obeyed, making his way through the back streets as the young woman had done, but Zeke stayed behind.

'I ain't got many years,' he said, 'come on, soldier.' Leaning on the old man in such a manner that it was a wonder Zeke did not collapse under the not inconsiderable weight of his companion, Carter limped along and they followed Tom.

They did not have much time to make their escape because they could hear shouting and yelling behind them as the cowboys who had handled the battering ram gathered at the foot of the ladder. It would take just one of them to climb up and see that they were gone, work out what had happened and shoot them in their retreating backs.

That was when the owner of the laundry appeared. Mr Ping stood before Zeke and Carter, held up a restraining hand and bundled them – with the help of his co-workers – into the back of the building.

'Door out other side,' he told them. This meant that they were away from the streets and could not be tracked as effectively. 'You stay in, lie low?' asked the owner.

'No,' said Carter, 'this'll be the first place they search if we've vanished.' They were guided swiftly through the building, picking up a vague impression of a big fire pit where a cauldron was always kept boiling as a source of water for the laundry, big wooden tubs with foaming soap, thick wooden poles and bundles of clothing sitting on racks, before coming to the side door of the building.

The shouts and yells from further along the street had not diminished, but Carter knew the town intimately and had a mental map of where they could go. If they could get to the livery and sequester a couple of horses they could get away swiftly and live to fight another day. He was not hobbling as badly now and felt he could get to the building. They would risk coming out of the side alley and running along the boardwalk to the one place that would provide their means of escape. As they left the laundry Mr Ping put the palms of his hands together and gave them a little bow. Carter gave his saviour a nod and a grateful glance before the door closed.

Carter recovered some of his strength and he had lost none of his determination. 'We get out and run down the boardwalk,' he said, 'they won't be expecting us, we get our horses and we ride out of here.' They emerged from the alley in which they were standing and carried out the first part of his plan. The only trouble was, as they emerged a horseman came riding across the wide dirt track of the street. It was young Ralph, who had his leg strapped up and must have needed help getting into his big cowboy saddle. He came riding hard towards the two refugees with a furious expression on his face.

'I told Pops you would find a way to sneak out like the

rat you are, this is personal.' His words were a worry, because although he held the reins in one hand there was a Remington pistol in the other and he had a wild look in his eyes that argued this was a personal revenge. He drew a bead on Carter, who decided quickly that he was not going to kill the son of the most powerful man in the district. Instead he fired one of his own guns and the bullet sang between the horse's ears at close range. The animal, a skittish looking thoroughbred, deep chestnut in colour, had the nervous disposition of such animals and did not take kindly to a bullet coming so close that it seared some of the hair on its head. It gave a loud whinny, spun around and charged off down the street. Ralph had to drop his gun, grab both reins and hold on for his life as the animal made off into the distance.

'Good shooting,' said Zeke, but like his friend they did not stop to admire their work and began hurrying onwards. The problem was that their little fracas had attracted attention from further along the road. Knott had seen what had happened to his son and was in rapid pursuit, and from the look on his face and the guns in his hand it was obvious that he thought they had done him a favour by coming out into the open.

By this time they were close enough to the livery to duck down the side of the building even if they were not able to reach the entry. Carter pushed the old man into the space beside the wall, ducked in with him and turned. They were facing the side of the livery now, but there was a dead end where the foot of the alley had been blocked by a brick wall. There was a reason for this, as it acted as a deterrent for horse thieves, who might have led the animals out that way.

In a few short seconds Knott and his men would arrive and they would be under siege once more. Carter ducked out of the alleyway and fired a couple of times at random, not really having a chance to take aim before ducking back into shelter. This drew a flurry of shots in his direction and he knew that the end was inevitable. He no longer cared.

'Kill me if you want,' he said, 'but leave the old man alone, and don't go near the girl or my deputy!' The look on his face told its own story; the skin around his eyes was tight and his mouth was a grim line, his normal good nature missing from his whole manner. They could take him down but they were never, in the end, going to win, he would make sure of that.

Then he heard a sound that was quite different from the shouts and yells of those who were coming to get him. It was the regular sound of horses tearing up the hard, dusty ground as they thundered around the curve of the main street. To his astonishment, as he looked out of the alley, he saw two riders pass, followed by another six. The two riders in the lead were Tom and Rebecca and they were both armed and ready for action. The other six were large, grim-faced men who also bore arms. They were dressed in various types of clothing, but had a look of unity that showed they all belonged to the same profession. The horses of the six men came to a halt square with the alleyway and Carter immediately knew what to do. He ran out and stood between two of the creatures and the men who sat on them.

Knott and his remaining men were ranged out across the road, Knott with an expression on his face that argued he was in a mood to fire upon them, a thought tempered

154

by their numbers.

Tom looked at the men who had tried to free the prisoners and spoke in a fierce voice.

'You're all under arrest.'

'Yes, and before you start,' said Rebecca, 'these men with me are US Marshals, if you shoot on them you will be guilty of treason and you'll all hang.' This was more than enough for the cowboys who had made up Knott's force. Those who had hung back promptly vanished along the curve of the street and ran off as hard as they could. The remainder were arrested as the marshals dismounted, walked forward and took them into custody. Carter walked with them, a plea in his voice.

'Let me do this,' he said, and Rebecca nodded to the men, who fell back as he marched forward and grabbed the mayor, smacking the useless guns out of his hands. As they fell they opened and he realised the chambers were empty. Once more, Knott, always the politician had been relying on his men to kill the so-called outlaw sheriff.

'I am arresting you for many offences,' he said, 'including attempting to kill the sheriff of Destiny, or ordering your men to do so.' Rebecca came forward and flashed a card at Knott.

'And I am adding charges of election rigging,' she said, 'on behalf of Pinkerton's detective agency.'

The cells were full that night.

CHAPTER EIGHTEEN

John Carter looked up as the door of his cell was opened by the turnkey. He was soon in front of the judge in the County Court in Wichita. Judge Hodgson was well-known as one of the most severe to sit on the bench and he listened to the evidence against Carter with interest. He had already directed the jury accordingly, an assortment of men and women unknown to the accused man. They were back from retirement and returned a verdict of 'not guilty,' partly based on the fact that Carter had done what he needed to do in two earlier trials where he had given evidence that had made sure Jim Knott had been put in prison for a very long time, while his men Burrows and Lambert had been condemned to hang along with others. Only his money and a good lawyer had saved Jim Knott from the same fate.

Carter walked out of the court room a free man, jamming his hat down on his head as he did so, and avoiding the reporters from the local newspapers by simply drifting off to one side of the classically designed building and walking off swiftly before they could catch up with him.

Rebecca was waiting for him in a house belonging to her relatives in the middle of town. They had known that if he was released there would be a lot of attention directed towards them both. It was her testimony that had more or less freed him, and she had left the court while the jury deliberated because she could not bear to be there when the case was decided, even though it was almost a foregone conclusion. With the peppery nature of judges and the way they instructed the jury she could never be sure.

'You made it,' she said. 'I'm so glad I telegraphed the US marshals before I went off to join Zeke at his ranch. They were waiting in the next town, and before the siege, when you thought I was just changing, I telegraphed them to come over as fast as they could. I met them just outside town with Tom in tow.'

'Yep,' he had taken his hat off and was standing in the hall of the building with her, but he had not moved any further and his expression was sombre.

'I would have thought you would be delighted,' she said.

'Might be the case,' he said, 'except for the way it's turned out.'

'You can go back to your job now,' she said, and then she paused and looked at him. 'Don't you know?'

'Know what?'

'We investigated your election results too. Jim Knott was a twister all right, how he escaped the rope I don't know, but he let you believe you were rigged to win as well. Not the case, Johnny, you were elected by popular choice, everyone liked you.'

'I guess so.' Other men might have whooped with joy at this news, but he looked only mildly interested. 'Don't solve my problem, Becky. They're all against me now, all the businesses helped by Knott, his remaining men, Marty Hogan – he didn't get charged with complicity, but it was a near thing and it was his boy Elias who tried to kill me that day from a rooftop. The ordinary folks might like me, but as far as Destiny goes, I'm finished.'

'Surely you can go back to your job?'

'Nope, it would cause more trouble than it would solve. Knott's son is still out there, even though he was the one who tried to murder me, he's thirsting for revenge. That's it, there's no hope for me,' he brightened up a little. 'Still the good news, from what I hear is that Tom's in a good position and he'll get the job. He'll be re-elected too. I'll sneak in and see him soon – and the baby too, but I'm finished there.'

'What are you going to do?'

'I guess I'll light out to Texas, plenty of work there for a man who's willing to do a bit of law enforcement. I can maybe get a job with one of the rail companies as a detective, or go on the trail . . . there's a lot I can do.'

'Or you could stay here,' her face lit up with a mischievous smile and she came forward and kissed him.

'Not a good idea, not if you're going to be running Zeke's ranch.'

'Don't you know?'

'I ain't heard much in the last few days.'

'Zeke passed away last night.'

'What?'

'He was staying here; he said he'd never had so much

luxury in all his life, a real bed with a feather mattress. He went upstairs, lay down and never got up again, just kind of faded away. I spoke to him hours before, he was really happy that he had testified on your behalf.'

'I'm real sorry to hear this, he was a fighter.'

'I think he died happy, we'll be going to his funeral soon, and you'll be there. As for the ranch, I'm going to sell it as a going concern – to the Sullivans – and neither Knott nor Hogan will dare make a bid. He left everything to me, you know,' she smiled and kissed him again. 'I have something to show you.' She led him through to the front room. There was a teak desk there that seemed to glow in the sunlight that glanced through the shutter windows. 'I paid for it to be brought here; you really did earn it after all.'

He caressed the desk as if it was a living thing.

'I don't know what to say.'

'You're a good man, John Carter. If you think I'm going to let you go you're mistaken, but I know a man needs to work. How would you like a job with us?'

'Us?' he looked as if he was in a faint daze.

'Pinkerton's, we're always on the lookout for good people, and whatever else you might have done – and only with the best intentions – you're dogged, a survivor, and above all you're likeable as hell. You'll be an asset to the business.'

'No use, if I'm around here.'

'That's the best of it, you'll be sent on assignment, you can be based anywhere you want. What do you say?' He looked at her for a while, then for the first time since meeting her at the rendezvous he smiled and the good humour returned to his face.

'I say yes.'

They embraced again and set off to plan their new lives together.